# Praise for M. L. Newman's
# Fade Away Series

I0553217

## Fade Away

## A Kiss To Remember

"Fade Away had me on the edge of my seat wanting more…"
*-Steve P*

"Such a fun book! You can put me down on the pre-order list for the sequel."
*-Anthony*

"Can't wait to read the next book in this series."
*-Michael S*

"I was excited to get this book and it didn't disappoint."
*-Cyd D*

"This is a great story driven by fresh ideas and some great writing!"
*-Suzie*

Also By M. L. Newman

The Breeze Series
*My Night Breeze*
*Winds of Change*

The Hope Trilogy
*Glimmer of Hope*
*Hope Has A Glare*

*Blowing The Whistle*

# Far, Far Away

### (Fade Away, Book 2)

## A Friend of Regret

# M. L. Newman

WILLIAM COLLINS

PUBLISHED BY:
M. L. Newman Publishing

Copyright © 2016 by Ashley Newman
U.K., U.S.A., Canada

Editing services provided by LoriAnn Wale
Cover Design provided by Justin Janusaitis

More information can be found at the author's website http:// mlnewmanauthor.com/
ISBN-13: 978-0692798102
ISBN-10: 0692798102

Dedicated to my amazing Writers' Group!
*Thank you for all of your support during the writing process*

# Far, Far Away

# Table of Contents

# Prologue

Senior year of college was daunting enough between the normal stresses of midterms and finals, not to mention the impending graduation into adulthood. A seemingly random assault she suffered on campus had changed Lauren in more ways than just into a Sanguis Bellator, a blood-thirsty monster.

Her social life, once full of friends and activities, had plummeted to consist of the three people who knew what she had become. Taylor, the only one who had been there that night and tried to protect her from the assault, her best friend and safe haven. Quinn, her ex-boyfriend who dabbled in the sciences of Sanguis Bellator life. And Fallon, a real life campus protector who constantly threatened to take her out, presuming she was a danger to humanity. Whoever said life is what you make it was insanely disturbed.

The attacks on campus had slowed down to a trickle after her assault, but not because the creatures had disappeared. They were instead focused solely on her because, as it turned out, she was no common Bellator. Lauren was special and coveted, yet she didn't know exactly why. She had ignored their attempts to reach out to her to join them, trying to pretend their existence was a fairy tale to keep little kids in line. The result: to be taken against her will, waking up scared and injured.

# Chapter One

The tinted sunlight only barely lit the room. The walls were textured in coarse material that resembled dull marble, while the floor was a dark wood that creaked from time to time. Noises echoed easily through the walls from heavy footsteps to loud whispers. Even the door that kept her locked within couldn't hinder the noises from slipping through the cracks like it was part of their master plan all along.

Lauren lay on the makeshift bed, the mattress filled with too little cotton and too much hay that she felt stab her when she moved too much. Her leg, propped up above the blankets, felt extra dry and itchy from Bellator remedies to help it to heal.

She couldn't stop thinking about the night that they'd kidnapped her. Her mind had been clouded with preparing for finals, ignoring the pain she felt in her heart from being rejected by her best friend—and one-time lover—Taylor. Needless to say, she had been distracted when Quinn, her ex-boyfriend and current Bellator 'doctor,' had called her cell phone a few times in the middle of the night. When she called him back and he hadn't answered, she'd gone to check on him only to find their dilapidated Science Building, and occasional experiment headquarters, engulfed in flames.

Timing had been on her side. She had managed to get Quinn free from debris that had collapsed on him with the help of his current girlfriend, Fallon. They had been able to get out with his Bellator research data safely intact. Unfortunately, "Mousey," a lab mouse on which Quinn experimented with Lauren's Bellator blood, had been caught inside the building, and with her heart in her mouth, she went back into the building to find her furry friend. She had only managed to get him safely out just in the nick of time, wounding her leg in the process, as the integrity of the building buckled.

That was when Elijah had snatched her.

The only hint of company was a soft shuffle she could just barely hear before the locks released and the door opened, wafting in cooler air from the hallway.

"It is only me. Barbara," the female said, coming to Lauren's side only to gently push her back down onto the bed. "There's no need to excite yourself."

Lauren grit her teeth. Speaking was a waste of breath; no one had listened to her anyway. She could feel the cool gelatinous substance against her skin. All she could do was sigh and wait for Barbara to leave.

"Hmmm... Are you hungry, dear?"

Lauren shook her head.

"It would be best if you fed anyway. You're not healing very well," Barbara advised, gently pulling off the blindfold. "Just a snack if you're not ready for a whole meal then."

The room was blurry as Lauren's eyes adjusted again. She had to cherish what little amount of time she had with the blindfold removed; she only got this chance twice a day. Her eyes swept the room, noting a strange new addition against the wall. She squinted until it came into focus.

Light green eyes stared back hidden behind bushy dark brown eyebrows. His arms were thick with muscles protruding within his dutiful stance. He refused to speak, like a natural statue to be discovered by tourists. His stare took in her every breath like he'd be tested on it later. Maybe he would.

Barbara came back in dressed as usual in her business casual slacks and blazer; only today it was with a leash in her hand. When she tugged on it, a young man on was the other end. He could have been a peer, but she didn't recognize him. His hands were bound in front of him with the leash hooked into it. His frantic brown eyes searched the room as Barbara grabbed a handful of his dark hair, shoving him to the ground. His clothing wasn't expensive, but he appeared to be well taken care of, or at least as much as a human drinking fountain could be.

"Take as much as you need," Barbara encouraged, standing behind him.

"I'm not hungry," Lauren rasped.

"You haven't had anything since you've been here. Of course you are," Barbara stated, grabbing the man's arm as an offering. "No need to be modest."

"No."

"Don't be stubborn," Elijah stated, grabbing the young man's arm roughly, almost ripping it from his arm socket. The young man cried out in pain and fear. Lauren shrieked in reaction, trying to scramble from the bed, only to fall to the floor with her injured leg. Her hands, too, were bound before her as she used her good leg to push away from them.

Elijah easily grabbed her up as her shrieks hit another pitch higher. "Stop it. Calm down."

"No!" she hollered, thrashing within his arms until she began to choke.

He held her right side up, almost cradling her like a small child as she continued to cough until dark life force smeared her lips.

"Calm yourself. Lauren, relax," he said, trying to settle her back on the bed.

Lauren managed to get her coughing under control only to dry sob. "Please leave me alone to fade away on my own."

Barbara stopped, completely horrified by Lauren's words. Elijah frowned severely, grabbing the young man by the back of the shirt on his way out. Lauren could hear the soft shuffle of Barbara's feet before she heard the door shut and the lock engage.

*****

"She is unmanageable," a raspy voice declared. "Her instincts are non-existent."

Lauren checked the door but no one had come in. No one was talking to her directly, but clearly someone was talking about her. As far as she could tell, she and Barbara were the only ones there. She couldn't be sure who was speaking in the hall but had a guess.

"No, she is dishonorable. Has no—" The silence lengthened for a short time. "I understand. When will you arrive?"

Panic bubbled up as she sensed a change coming. Whatever happened, she certainly wasn't in a good place. She looked around the room, thankful that Barbara had forgotten to put the blindfold back on, trying to think of a way out of the binding on her hands. The room itself was scarce of furniture other than the bed she lay on. There were no mirrors or dresser, not even a closet. She pulled herself up from the bed, careful not to send any jolts of pain through the injured leg as she went over to the window.

She couldn't see much through the warped tint and could imagine it would only get worse throughout the winter season. The latches to lock and unlock the window were missing, leaving her to believe that it was never meant to open at all. She banged her bound wrists to the glass as if it would easily give way. No such luck. How could she possibly leave a room with only one way in and one way out?

"You're supposed to be in bed," Elijah stated.

Lauren hung her head, allowing it to press against the cool of the glass. "No, I'm supposed to be in class."

His heavy boots sounded behind her. "Are you going to get back in bed, or do I have to put you there?"

"I'm not a rag doll. I can take care of myself," she groused.

Silence echoed behind her. His presence alone was loud enough to eclipse her vocal complaints. With her lips smashed together, keeping in her protests, she took her time getting back on the bed. Taking care to prop her leg back up as per usual, she was well aware of being watched closely. He kept his distance of at least a few feet as his eyes scanned her thoroughly. Maybe he had a mental checklist he was going through.

"Do you understand what you're doing here? Why you're here at all?"

"You kidnapped me." She glared at him.

Elijah scoffed at the accusation. "Your place is here with the rest of the Bellator family."

"Family?! If this is how you treat each other then I want no part of it. In fact, consider me gone," she said, looking towards the door.

"Your place is *here*," he repeated firmly. "You're not going anywhere."

"My place is with kidnappers and stalkers?"

"Raeffe would have no qualms about grabbing someone you cared about to make a point. He is ruthless and determined. Remember that the next time you even think to spout off at him," he warned. "You're in enough trouble as it is."

Lauren eyed the door longingly until he blocked it from view. "The king is coming—"

"King?" Lauren interrupted.

Elijah nodded. "Yes, King Erebus, and he is here to see *you*."

Her eyes refused to blink as she stared into his green eyes, fear filling her again. "To see me?"

"The last time he came was to execute a traitor. Trust me when I say this is highly unusual."

Elijah went to the door, throwing her one last look as she frantically tried to gain her thoughts. "He can be your savior or your enemy."

# Chapter Two

Piercing screams seeped through her dreams easily. The abrupt pitch caught her off guard, sending her to the floor where the pitch only heightened before being cut off just as suddenly. Lauren was shaken to the core as she panted. Her mind fluttered to make sense of where she was, let alone what she had heard.

Terrified, she began trying to get up from the floor as heavy footfalls sounded in the hallway. Was someone coming for her now? Elijah's words had already done their worst on her dreams, but now it seemed reality was catching up with her. She frantically grabbed at the makeshift bed, trying to put herself in a better position to protect herself just as the footfall stopped at her door.

She cringed in silence, waiting for the door to swing open. She was certain there would be at least three Bellators ready to take her down, not including Raeffe who would be watching happily. Whatever torture method they would use upon her would be too much to handle. Her parents hadn't even spanked her growing up, and they loved her. These monsters had no feelings towards her at all.

Her hazel eyes widened as she watched the handle begin to turn. She gripped her bound hands into fists as she leaned against the bed to support herself. She wouldn't make it easy on them. She was a handful to mess with, and they would remember her; she would leave her mark on them.

Just as the door began to push open, it stopped, pulling shut with a release of the knob.

*****

Lauren stared up at the ceiling hopelessly. Sleep had evaded her the majority of the night, leaving her feeling exhausted and wired all at once. The sound of the door creaking open gave her such a fright that she'd gasped hard enough to start a coughing frenzy. Barbara came to her side, patting her back and removing the binding from her wrists until Lauren caught her breath.

Barbara's fingers delicately pulled up the fabric, checking her wounded leg. The cold gel put upon the injury sent a shiver through her system.

"Finally, it's starting to heal up properly," Barbara commented. "Although, it would have already had you fed like a good girl."

"No," Lauren said as sternly as she could manage.

"Well, despite your own efforts, it does look better," Barbara admitted cautiously. "How about a small snack? It does get easier, I promise."

Lauren rolled away from her, facing the wall. She was too tired to bother speaking up. The sound of the door opening and closing behind her only made her feel worse. It was as if her organs were indeed struggling to keep her conscious. She covered her face with her hands as a quivering sob began to leak out. She took a deep breath, but pain filled her chest, making her feel worse, as she sounded an even louder sob to bounce back from the walls.

All she wanted was to be safely back in her bed on campus. Even if she wasn't really speaking to Taylor, just having a comfortable place to rest was worth it. She thought of her warm blankets that she'd picked with her mom the summer before her freshman year. It was a memory that she hadn't appreciated until now while she was lying on the rough makeshift bedding where bits of straw were actually sticking into her back and sides.

Was it too much to ask that she be able to get out a good cry? Even if it wouldn't practically help her situation, it would leave relief in its wake. Her body continued to heave out the awkward sobs that kept her face dry until she was shaking violently.

"Stop it," Elijah commanded suddenly from behind her, shaking her. His eyes bored into hers intensely with no indication of understanding. "*Weakness is not tolerated.*"

"Why do you even care?" she spat back. "I'm as good as dead."

Elijah stood before her in the formal stance she recognized. The only change she noticed was the stare that was so intense it jostled her thoughts. "I've watched your interactions for months. How, even when you were stabbed by Fallon, you didn't kill her."

Lauren's thoughts flicked back to that day a few weeks ago when Fallon had shoved a dagger under her ribs without remorse. Fallon had claimed it to be an accident. While Lauren had eventually believed that it was an accident, she already knew not to trust her and she had pushed back for survival. That same night, Lauren had been given a Bellator keepsake, an old fashioned lantern from the 1800s. Maybe Fallon had seen the Bellator leaving the scene and mistook Lauren for him. She couldn't be sure.

Lauren's eyes widened. "What? Fallon? Do you know her—?"

"I also personally watched you endanger your entire being to save a small creature that was caged," he stated, cutting her off. "I don't know any other being, human or not, who would do that. Maybe there is something worth saving in you. You were changed with a purpose whether you know it or not."

*****

Loud footsteps sounded on the other side of the door as the only warning. She sat up just as Raeffe filled the doorway. His serious expression welcomed her. Without saying a word, he went to the end of the bed, grabbing the fabric up and out of the way to stare at her wound. His forehead crinkled for a long moment before he stared directly at her. When he glanced back at the wound, his teeth gritted loudly enough for her to hear.

Barbara quietly entered the room with her usual curing remedy. Raeffe stepped aside, watching Barbara apply the gel.

"Nothing?" Raeffe asked Barbara.

Barbara shook her heard in response as she cleaned up the area of the wound before tugging the fabric down to protect it. Raeffe stared at Lauren again, this time with less scrutiny but more curiosity in his eyes. Whatever he was looking for seemed to elude him. His frustrated eyes became dark slits before he exited the room.

"What was that about?" Lauren asked.

"Procedure," Barbara said matter-of-factly. "Snack?"

Lauren was ready to spit out a quick 'no' when a thought stopped her. "Maybe, if you tell me."

Barbara's eyes widened, showing off the black veins surrounding the irises. "You're hungry?"

"I'm not sure. What did Raeffe mean?"

Barbara's mouth pinched unwillingly for a minute. She turned away from Lauren and headed for the door. Lauren was sure she had lost the chance to get some answers when Barbara shut the door and turned towards her. "Will you feed?"

Lauren wanted to nod just to get answers, but the idea of actually drinking blood made her feel queasy. Especially the blood of some stranger. She didn't imagine the Bellators asking for donations to get the blood they drank, which tainted any chance of her wanting a drop of it. The fear the Bellator would have instilled in the poor human before taking their life completely was repugnant to her. She did all she could to forget the memory of tasting Taylor. He was the exception; he always had been.

Barbara assessed her reactions from the door, clearly unamused by the delay. "We don't waste food here. What you're asking for is not negotiable."

Lauren lay back down, frustrated, staring at the ceiling, waiting to hear the door shut.

"No snack then?"

Lauren ignored her question. "When is Elijah coming?"

Barbara sighed hard enough for it to come across as a sucker punch to Lauren's gut. "Elijah is on a mission. He won't be coming. And he certainly won't be discussing anything with *you*."

The distaste was clear in Barbara's voice. It matched the expression on her face before she left, shutting the door behind her.

*****

Barbara was accurate when she said that Elijah wouldn't be coming by that day. Nor had he come by the next. As much as Lauren didn't care for any of them, he was somewhat... tolerable. He spoke to her like she existed. Barbara treated her like a starving animal, which was ludicrous. Lauren had only begun to think about her friends and family back home when the door swung open. Raeffe entered with the most genuine smile she'd ever witnessed. It reached his dark eyes, allowing them to seem welcoming and even joyous.

"Lauren, it is time," he said in the calmest voice.

*Time for what?*

As she leaned forward, using her hands to grip the edge of the makeshift bed to stand, she noticed two Bellators in the hallway. From their expressionless faces, there was no hint as to what—or who—was waiting for her. She walked carefully towards them, feeling more confident that her leg wasn't protesting too badly, but her anxiety was setting off alarms everywhere in her mind.

Raeffe closed the door behind her, heading down the long hallway where the lower half of the wall was wood paneled and the top was painted white. When she reached the stairs on her cautious trip, a shiver went through her at the thought of going down them. One of the Bellators wasted no time

24

grabbing her up in his arms, albeit as carefully as he could manage while catching her off guard. When his feet reached the bottom step, he continued down another hall that was lit by small sconces. The third door on the left opened up as Raeffe arrived; however, the other Bellators stopped.

Lauren wiggled in her guard's arms, trying to be put down. He didn't flinch for a second, only repositioned her until it was more comfortable for him to hold her. She sighed heavily in complaint to deaf ears. After a moment, a voice spoke in a language she didn't understand, sending one Bellator inside as she was carried in behind.

The room was structured with beautiful tapestries adorning the walls in bright purples and greens. Bellators lined up against the walls. There were six on each side parallel to an overly cushioned love seat where Erebus sat. There was no mistaking him for anyone else. His eyes were a hauntingly beautiful pale blue, and his hair was short and blond. His face was clear of blemish or scar, with cheekbones sharp enough to pierce skin. He sat still with a look of unwilling patience as she was set down on her feet.

Lauren brushed her ash blond hair back from her face as Raeffe took his place beside the couch. She knew better than to speak first, but the silence was making her uneasy. Her eyes scanned towards the left noticing Barbara, the only other female in the room. She glanced towards the right and noticed Elijah, the next closest to Raeffe and Erebus. His expression was serious as he stared at nothing in front of him.

"Lauren, is it?" Erebus questioned with a velvety smooth voice.

She nodded, unsure if she was allowed to speak.

"I've heard so much about you already. I feel like I know you," he said in a manner that walked the fine line between welcoming and menacing.

Lauren blinked at him, unsure of a response. Certainly, she didn't want to make him angry.

"What is the purpose of your existence?" he asked.

Swallowing hard, she wracked her brain for an answer. The purpose she wanted was to have a career where she could travel to look at historical pieces all over the world. Maybe work at a museum someday. Maybe get married and have kids... None of those applied anymore, though. She had no purpose that she could think of in a state like this.

"Anything," she said.

"Anything what?"

"I can be purposeful for anything," she said quietly.

His eyes sent a shiver through her as she watched him assess her words. She obviously hadn't answered in a way he expected, but maybe the answer didn't matter. He wanted to hear her, so she spoke.

"She finds solace in her old life," Raeffe said, staring at her. "Allowing humans to brainwash her to turn her back on her own kind."

Erebus rubbed a hand over his jawline as he looked toward Raeffe reflectively before he turned his attention back on Lauren. "Do you wish to die? Would that be easier for you?"

Lauren shook her head slowly, declining to verbally answer his question as fear had grit her teeth shut.

"Certainly, we can't have you roaming around on your own, putting our way of existence at risk by your actions," Erebus said with a heavy sigh, weighted with tiredness. "It's a shame. You're the only female who's changed successfully since Barbara here."

Lauren wanted to protest to save her own life, but what could she say to get them to listen? Would they listen to her if she truly said what she needed to? "I haven't tried to—"

"She protects *humans*. Ignoring her fellow Bellators' needs. She is a traitor," Raeffe seethed.

The words barely left his lips as two Bellators appeared at her side, each grabbing one of her arms to keep her in place. She tried to tug her arms back and away from them but it was of no use. A shiny metal object was unwrapped by Raeffe, who was grinning from ear to ear. As he stepped closer, she realized it was shaped like a pear except with a metal stem.

Lauren fought with every ounce of strength she had within her, tugging to release her arms. Raeffe brought the shiny metal object towards her mouth.

Her eyes widened with fright, "No!"

She kicked him as hard as she could manage in his stomach, leveraging her body with the tension in her arms from the other two Bellators holding her up. The metal object clanked to the ground as she proceeded to scream and fight for her life as much as she could. She managed to loosen one arm out of one Bellator's grip but was quickly pulled into a bear hug by the other Bellator. She continued to fight and kick at any Bellator that attempted to come near her.

Raeffe picked up the metal object with not only anger at her offense but with the darkest evil look she'd ever seen in her life. She screamed as high pitched as she could, kicking until her body revolted, sending black life force at high velocity toward Raeffe. The projectile landed all over him as well as down her shirt. That was when she heard the voice of the true commander and king.

"Raeffe," Erebus said sternly as he stood from his seated area. "Step aside."

"King Erebus," Elijah spoke up. "May I?"

Erebus appraised Elijah intently before nodding and sitting back down himself. With a unique gracefulness that only Elijah could pull off, he went over towards Lauren who was still trying to recover. She kept wiggling within the Bellator's arms that held her tightly until Elijah reached her. The intensity that he had placed upon her previously was nothing compared to what he was doing to her now.

"Are you ill?" he asked.

"I don't know…"

"When did you last feed?" Elijah asked louder than needed in the quiet room.

"I haven't… I don't…" Lauren couldn't think straight as her words and thoughts became jumbled. "I haven't…"

"Barbara," Elijah beckoned for Erebus's benefit. "Has she fed since arriving?"

Barbara took a step forward to acknowledge the question. "She has not fed. She hasn't yet fully recovered from the fire."

"King Erebus, if you believe she deserves to be disciplined for her actions, I will continue with the pear of punishment," Elijah said, leaving judgment to the king.

*He could be your savior or your enemy.*

Lauren stared at Erebus with black life force smeared across her chin. She wouldn't appear as frail or weak, although she clearly was. She wouldn't give any of them the satisfaction of taking her out without a fight. If she was going to die, it would be her own choice at her own hand, not at anyone else's.

"Not feeding?" Erebus questioned aloud. "When the body isn't fed, the mind deteriorates." He nodded to himself for a moment. "We shall see where her loyalties lie…"

*****

Washed and changed into a t-shirt that wasn't covered in her life force, she was sent back to her room. She curled up into a ball beneath the thin blanket at the end of the bed, wishing to be anywhere else. Escaping this awful place would do little to help her current situation with threats being made against her friends. Honestly, where could they all go?

It wasn't too much later when Barbara came in with a small cup of

28

"lunch." She didn't bother asking her to eat. She placed it wordlessly beside the makeshift bed and left, shutting the door behind her. Lauren stayed bundled up, hoping for unconsciousness to take her away, even if it was only for a short while.

"Have you fed?" Elijah asked, closing the door behind him.

"I'm getting really sick of being asked," Lauren complained from beneath the blanket. "No."

"This doesn't have to be so hard. You could be free if you really wanted to be. Just try not to be such a burden all the time," Elijah advised.

Lauren chose that moment to tug the cover down to send him a meaningful glare.

"No one trusts you here. You're a risk."

"Why do you care?" she spat back at him.

"I don't."

She sat up to stare at him then when he pointed toward his ears and then towards the door. They were being listened to. It was starting to make sense. Erebus had granted her a chance to prove herself but nothing else.

*****

A few awkward days had passed when Erebus requested her presence alone. The Bellators escorted her like last time, except her leg was no longer a main concern. Much to her own liking, there was no need for anyone to touch her as she went into the big living room area. Erebus sat on his "throne" as she stood before him like last time.

"Have you found your purpose?" Erebus asked.

Lauren took a deep breath and repeated what she'd practiced with Elijah. "I'm still learning about this way of existence."

She could tell by the downturn of his mouth that he didn't much care for the answer. "And how do you plan to learn?"

"I don't know much of anything about what to expect. Looking at it from my experience, wanting to stay this way at all has been tainted. However, if I were to learn from you all, I could learn what it truly means to be a Bellator."

Erebus sat back in his chair, crossing his leg over with feigned interest. "Why do you think that you are different from the others?"

*Different?*

Lauren looked directly in his eyes so he could see the truth within her statement. "I'm not different, just uneducated."

"Raeffe!" Erebus called. "She is to spend time outside of her holding cell to learn. She is to be escorted at all times, and only for a few hours at a time."

# Chapter Three

She stared outside of her window, the trees covered in snow with no hint of disruption. What she wouldn't give to feel fresh air against her skin. Part of her knew it was a lie; the air wasn't truly what she was looking for. If she were allowed one step outside of this hell, she'd take off without looking back...

That wasn't exactly smart, either. She still had to worry about the safety of her friends and family. She'd have to check with Elijah to see if she'd been followed home at any time while she was being observed previously, if they knew where she lived with her parents. If her family were off the radar, then she only had to think of her friends on campus. Not easier in the least.

Her human, clueless friends, like Hilary and Gina, would have to be forgotten. She couldn't just whisk them away to some faraway place. They would quickly understand that she was different, and while the knowledge would prepare them to know what to expect from a Bellator, it wouldn't save them from an attack. And Quinn and Fallon were a complete island on their own. They weren't her friends. Quinn was a huge help when it came to understanding the mechanics of being a Bellator, but there was no way he would make it in a battle. Not without Fallon's help.

Lauren sighed heavily at the thought of having to deal with Fallon for any length of time. She could be bearable in small doses with Quinn as a buffer, maybe; but not long term like it might become. Lauren thought back to Elijah's mention of her. He admitted to following her around campus. Did he know all of her friends? Was he a friend? She doubted it.

The only human left to consider was Taylor...

She turned at the sound of door opening. Barbara was delivering a small cup of "dinner," placing it beside the makeshift bed. Lauren studied her docile state. It seemed so out of character compared to her and the others.

"Barbara," Lauren began, "what's your purpose here?"

The brittle smile held its odd place. "I support the nest and the warriors."

31

"Like a family?"

Barbara shook her head. "No, my dear, we are much more than any human memory you may have."

"How so?"

"Families have a home. This is a nest," she clarified. "There is no home here, not even for me."

Lauren stayed silent, trying to think that through. *A life where there is no home... what does that feel like?* She'd considered her home with her parents, but soon that would have changed with her getting her own place after graduation. Which brought her to another thought.

"What about a husband? Is there no future to grow?"

"We are a community only. It is uncommon for a warrior to stray from the only life we know," Barbara advised. She looked back at the small cup with an encouragement. "Please think of your importance through all of this. Dare I say, it has been three decades since a young woman successfully transitioned."

*****

Lauren thought back to the last time she'd spoken to Taylor. Being rejected by him seemed minuscule compared to where she was now. She wondered if he'd known how she felt, if he could see the calmness that was unleashed afterward. She couldn't deny that she loved him. That was the only reason she'd stayed in this awful state. Having him accept her and even take her to bed was confirmation that she was worth trying for. Even if she was a monster. She wanted to cry again, if her body would just allow her the satisfaction.

Maybe it was reality hitting that there was a strong chance that she'd never see him again, never get the chance to say the words herself. That choked her as she lay down, hoping for a chance to one day say all the things she needed to, even if it meant being rejected again. Taylor deserved to hear the words from someone who meant them.

*****

The door opened as two Bellators stepped inside. They were the same ones who had initially taken her to see Erebus. She followed them out into the hall wordlessly. She could be grateful only that her leg was feeling better, and she wouldn't have to deal with them rushing her too much.

They went downstairs and into another section of the nest. The hallway was shorter with only two doors. She entered, following the Bellators into a spacious room where three other warriors waited. Barbara came through a side door towards the back of the room with her hands full of material. She placed it on the table before calling Lauren over to her side.

"I need these sorted by size," Barbara advised as she beckoned to the first warrior. Without having to ask, she grabbed a shirt and jacket for him. He nodded respectfully before heading out of the room.

Lauren looked through the clothes on the table and was startled to notice how different they were. There were brands she easily recognized from her own shopping adventures mixed with a few dated ones. She complied with her instructions, putting them in order from medium to extra large as Bellators came by depleting the piles. By the fourth round of warriors, she was restocking new materials onto the table as Elijah caught her attention.

He stood stoically, his attention on the task at hand without acknowledging her. She could feel the subtle signs of relaxation in her tensed muscles upon seeing him. Her thoughts clouded her judgment when she thought about him. *He's not a friend by any means, but again, I can't see him as an enemy, either. Am I that desperate for comfort to accept his odd presence as it is?*

Lauren cleared her mind as she began organizing more fabric bundles on the table when a curious dark stain caught her attention. It wasn't very big at all, and as she looked closer, the item had another and another. Three small drops that were rough to the touch stared back at her.

"Where did you get these?" Lauren asked Barbara.

"The resources that we get are reused and repurposed," Barbara said.

Lauren's fingers pulled back from the stained fabric as she realized what it was. As she looked at the clothes before her, her stomach rumbled a complaint of queasiness. They had belonged to countless victims. Without a second thought, Lauren blurred into the hallway with her hand over her mouth. She tried to clear her mind of thoughts and breathe through her nose slowly. She couldn't change the past, and she certainly needed to get a grip. This was a test, and if she couldn't hack it...

"Are you ill?" Barbara asked from behind her.

Lauren shook her head. "I'm fine. What's next?"

Barbara eyed her suspiciously. "I don't think—"

"Finished?" Raeffe asked, coming from down the hall.

*****

The room felt as though it had shrunk while she was gone. Maybe from her perspective it had been bigger when she hadn't spent such a long time outside of it in the main part of the nest. Knowing the rest of her evening would be spent trapped inside was making her feel worse.

"Why do you do this to people?" she heard herself ask aloud.

Raeffe sneered, "Why do humans have children?"

Lauren faced him. "Do you know who attacked me?"

Raeffe glared at the terminology, but she refused to back down. "Yes, I was *attacked*. I used to be happy before that psychopath savagely assaulted me

34

before taking off into the night. Those *evil humans* kept me in one piece."

"Well, it fits that you were the reason he never came back alive," he admitted roughly. "It wasn't long after he was advised of his mission to turn a female from your campus."

Lauren took in the information slowly as she remembered the night she'd followed Fallon from the cafeteria. She hadn't transitioned yet into a Sanguis Bellator and knew that Fallon had the information she needed to understand what was happening to her. Fallon had been surprised to see her, but Lauren made her loyalties clear by attacking the Bellator with Fallon. The Bellator made no plea towards her when she went after him. He knew exactly who she was. Not that it mattered; he took her down to the ground hard, ready to feed on her and end her life.

That Sanguis Bellator had no clue that Fallon would strike back so fast, taking advantage of his distraction with Lauren. Fallon planted her sharp knife right into his heart, and within seconds, he faded away for good.

So, Fallon had killed the warrior who made Lauren? Her eyes blinked a few times as she tried to think it through. She had no feelings towards the creature that night. Her mind had been focused on protecting the older woman and then helping Fallon. Was she supposed to know? Either way, it wouldn't help her now, and it didn't change anything. He was a monster who destroyed her human life.

Raeffe stood, watching her filter through her thoughts as coldness filled his features. "As careless as you feel towards his disappearance, it only proves that you're more like us than you think."

\*\*\*\*\*

That evening, Lauren was mid-pace near the window when Elijah came in with Barbara right behind him. She carried in a cup filled with "dinner," only it was a third of the size she usually brought. Maybe Barbara was giving up on her, after all. Lauren glanced up at Elijah, noticing his usual stance when they weren't alone.

As Barbara began to turn away, he too began to follow her. Lauren panicked, unable to help her reaction. "Elijah?"

His shoulders stiffened at the sound of his name. Had he expected her to let him just walk away? He was the only somewhat sane creature here that she could speak to. She wanted some type of answers from him. He understood what was going on here.

"Did you know," Lauren paused, noticing Barbara lingering at his side, "the guy who changed me?"

Elijah gave her one stiffened nod.

"And you knew about—"

"It was his mission," Elijah snapped, cutting her off. "He succeeded... even if he isn't around to know it."

Her eyes widened at his words. Did he know she played a role in his death? Would he think differently of her if he knew the truth? Clearly, she had the right to protect herself when he was attacking her and Fallon. She hadn't even transitioned into a full Bellator yet, and she'd taken one out with the help of a human. She could only hope that that stayed a secret. Raeffe would never accept that and would excitedly take that to Erebus to prepare her execution.

"Have you done it?" Lauren asked to fill in the silence, watching Barbara stay close to Elijah's side protectively. Maybe Barbara was the reason he wasn't coming around so much. She was worried about what Lauren could finagle from him.

"Yes, it has been my mission," he admitted. "One I take great pride in."

The tone in his voice matched his facial expression. There was no question as to his alliance, which only caused her to doubt her own instincts.

Elijah followed Barbara fully out of the room. It wasn't until the door clicked that Lauren's self-preservation inner voice began to speak up. *I can't stay here. I can't become one of them.*

*****

It had been six days of limited interactions between her and the warriors. Her "learning experiences" amounted to hands off and distant sightings of a few of them training while bringing linens through with Barbara. Since speaking with Elijah last, Barbara had given her behind the scenes jobs to keep the distance in place. Not that Lauren was in any way wishing to interact with him again now. He was making her head hurt with the mixed signals of helping her yet keeping her an arm's length away.

Only to make things interesting, she awoke on the seventh day to a bottle of pills beside her head. It was no ordinary bottle of pills; in fact, it was way too familiar. It was clearly from Quinn. How did that manage to find its way to her? Past everyone? She unscrewed the lid, finding nothing inside but the contents of the pills she expected. No note or hidden message within. Lauren hid the bottle within her pillowcase to decipher later.

The duty of her learning experience today was to once again assist the Bellators with fresh clothes and linens before they were to train for the day. Barbara seemed oddly occupied by the small task, so it took them both by surprise when Raeffe approached the table.

"Are you done with her?"

Barbara nodded with a curious look as he grunted for Lauren to follow. He made no attempt to speak to her directly, which made it easier in her opinion.

He led her into the training room where four Bellators were hard at work.

37

She watched one working on his strength technique with fascination and fear. The warrior was benching over a thousand pounds without even breaking a sweat. After the first set of reps, he added five hundred pounds to each side. Lauren had to look away; it was too much to take in and watch.

"How far?" questioned a particularly small warrior. He was only a few inches taller than Lauren, but his frame was broad with unmistakable muscle. His black curly hair made his facial features seem less threatening. He appeared relaxed like he'd just gotten back from tanning on a summer vacation. She knew better than to believe her own eyes.

"Just basics, Jon," Raeffe replied.

"Limits?"

Raeffe worked minimally to cover his smirk. "Push and find out."

The warrior's eyes took in Lauren with curiosity. "To the mats," Jon declared.

The other two Bellators were finishing up within the room and were now having a side conversation. Nervously, she followed Jon's instructions and stood as awkwardly as she felt. Whatever Raeffe had planned for her wasn't going to be a walk in the park. She took stock of Jon headed her way. Again, he didn't appear either threatening or inviting, just indifferent.

Suddenly, he was a blur of motion in front of her. She watched his coordinated steps in wonder until he was close enough to almost hit her. She stepped back, but he wouldn't relent, coming closer and closer until she had her back against the wall of the training room. What was she supposed to do? Fighting was one thing, but this wasn't fighting. It was more like a techno glow stick dance minus the glow sticks.

Lauren mimicked his hand motions poorly, causing the other Bellators to snicker. Whatever she was supposed to do, this wasn't it. Still, she continued trying to find the rhythm that he had until she matched him perfectly. The next portion was the foot work, not so easy when she needed to keep him in her sights. She took a few steps, awkwardly and off pace, causing her to check her hands and almost bumping into the Bellator before her. It wasn't until she stepped on his foot that he grunted, irritated.

"Sorry," she said before trying to pick up her rhythm again.

"This is not a dance." His attention was on her hips and feet. "You're swaying."

"Sorry," she apologized again, focusing on her hands and then taking a stiff step forward. She made sure that the only movement was her hands to the side and forward. He pushed her back by stepping toward her; she lost focus on her hand motion.

"Sorry—"

"Ten push-ups. Now," Jon demanded.

Lauren looked down to the mat and back up at him. He was serious. She hadn't done push-ups since high school, and even then they were mediocre. She glanced back towards the mat dubiously. A strange feeling of falling blew wisps of hair across her cheeks until she felt the mat stop her fall as she huffed.

"Fifteen for hesitation."

When she looked up from the floor, the other Bellators were making no qualms about hiding the pleasure they were getting out of this. She didn't bother trying to look at the one who shoved her down. He had enough trouble headed his way...

She placed her hands on the mat before setting her feet. Knowing herself all too well, as she went down, she blew out her breath and pushed back up with trembling arms. Trying to get it over with quickly would only cause more issues. Not that that would be a surprise. She went down again—this time, pushing up was an even bigger struggle.

Her arms were on fire and begging to relax. She'd only done two! How could she get to fifteen? The down was easy, she admitted to herself as she lowered. When she attempted to push back up, nothing happened. She was stuck in the lower position. She couldn't give up; she wouldn't give up. She thought of Fallon and the annoying way she'd pushed her buttons.

*"What do you want?"*

*"To be rich? Oh, you mean, from you," Fallon smirked. "Checking in for Quinn."*

*Lauren rolled her eyes at that. "Nothing has changed."*

*"Have you been feeding?"*

*"Is that all you're worried about? I'm not, so don't," she replied.*

*"You know what will happen if you don't. Not that I care."*

Lauren pushed back up in surprise and then down.

*"Next question," Lauren pushed.*

*"That's it."*

*Lauren stopped to look her straight in the eye. "What the hell is that? Quinn doesn't stop at just one question."*

*"What's the point in going on if you don't feed? Again, not that I care. In fact, I'm pretty glad to hear it."*

She pushed back up in irritable frustration and then down. She'd lost count on how many push-ups she'd done. And maybe that was the key. To forget the situation at hand and use what she had to her own benefit.

*"You bitch."*

*Fallon laughed carelessly. "Temper, temper. I'm only applauding you for doing what you say. How many times have you said you didn't want to hurt anyone? And look at you... keeping your word."*

As the memories continued, so did her effort, blocking out the pain until Jon stopped her. "Who are you talking to?"

Lauren stared up at the warrior in question. "What? I didn't say anything."

"I heard you," he said. "Stand up."

She did as she was told, not remembering having said a word. As he assessed her, his opinion stayed the same.

"Take her," Jon advised to one of the lingering Bellators.

# Chapter Four

Showered and sore, she sat on the end of the bed in disbelief. She couldn't wrap her mind around what she'd been put through. What was the purpose? She lay back in frustration, hitting her head on the bottle beneath the pillowcase. She'd forgotten all about it.

The door opened allowing Elijah quiet entry. Her guard instinctively rose until he shut the door fully behind him.

"Well?" he asked.

"Well what?"

"Did you take them?" he pushed.

"No, and I won't. Nice try, though."

Elijah grit his teeth as he spoke. "You're as stubborn as Quinn said."

"You spoke with him? When?" He had her attention now.

"The other night, I got him to answer your phone. I met him officially this morning."

Questions plundered her mind in quick succession. *What had they talked about? Where was this going? Did they believe Elijah wanted to help her situation?* The only proof was the bottle she now held within her hands. "What did he say?"

"He only confirmed what I already knew of your stubbornness. He even advised what your boyfriend did when you poisoned yourself," Elijah said.

*Quinn had said what?!* She was freaking out and with good reason. That was none of Elijah's business, nor was it right for Quinn to tell.

"I need you to understand one thing," he began. "No one here cares about you, other than whether or not you're a vital asset. That is the only saving grace you have."

Lauren understood that more than he could explain. Today was a test, but she had no idea if she'd failed or not. Would Elijah warn her, or stand by and watch her be killed? Instead of asking, she stood up, doing the hand motion that she was shown earlier. Elijah's eyebrow furrowed at her actions and shook his head.

"Your hips move too much. This isn't a dance," he stated.

"Can you teach me?"

He had her stand in the middle of the room with her hands poised in position. "Don't move your hands. You want to counter whatever advance I make."

"Like a duel?"

He nodded before lunging towards her, and she countered his steps. For every step he took towards her, she countered with a different angle of footwork to stay out of reach. It took a few tries before she felt the confidence to advance on him in return. This time, she added her hand motions to put it together.

"Less hip movement," he commented.

Lauren couldn't help the tiny movements even when she actively focused on them. Instead, she used it to her advantage to distract him, allowing her hands to tap his shoulder.

"What was that?"

"You win by making the connection in a duel. I don't have a sword, so I tapped," she explained.

"Was today your first day?"

"Yeah. They weren't impressed, either."

Elijah kept quiet for a minute. "How did you feel when you were watching Jon's demonstration?"

Lauren shrugged. "Nothing really. Fascinated? It reminds me of dancing... maybe that's why I can't stop doing the hip movements." She could almost see the questions forming in his eyes. "What?"

This time, he firmly declined any response, leaving only an open stare for her. His expression was mixed between the warrior who was loyal to his nest and the Elijah she knew when he let her in. Maybe he could feel the change, too? Had she been the connection to his human side that had been forgotten? There had to be more human emotion left within him; more than just the Bellator coldness he wore all of the time.

She could only imagine the person he was before the change. If he had family and friends whom he cared about and who missed him dearly. If they remembered him at all. Was he clinging to the nest for security of his own heart?

Even as she looked at him now, slowly returning to the warrior he protected himself within, there was something in his eyes she couldn't explain. A beauty that spoke to her, a pureness that allowed her to speak to him with respect.

"I must not be that bad since you keep visiting me," she whispered, half-seriously and half-jokingly.

"It's pretty taxing," he admitted.

She couldn't hide her smile even if she mashed her lips together. His lips lifted slightly at the corners in response. It was as close to a smile as she'd ever gotten out of him, and it was remarkable. He felt so familiar to her, not because of the time they'd spent together but something else. Like she knew him...

"Have we met before, Elijah?" she blurted out.

His eyebrows rose in alarm. "Why?"

"I can't," she whispered lowly, "shake this feeling like I've seen you before."

His face relaxed and his eyes softened again with a hint of humor. "I've been on that campus for years. You've probably seen me without realizing it."

Lauren thought about that, allowing her next question to slip out. "Were you there... that night... when I..."

"No."

Part of her wanted to ask if he would've turned her himself if it were his

44

mission. Seeing it through her own eyes wasn't easy. She wasn't an easy target with Taylor by her side. Any human attacker would have thought twice about trying them, but not a Bellator. Would Elijah have attacked her the very same way or waited until she was alone? Both scenarios were difficult to reason with. She wasn't special, though; he would have finished his mission by turning her. And it would have been a complete surprise to everyone that she had made it.

"He left me like this," she began.

"His name was Kevin. Something happened to him. It isn't protocol to leave," Elijah frowned intensely. "You were supposed to be brought into this slowly and trained before the full change."

"Is that why I'm getting more chances? 'Cause I was abandoned?"

He nodded stiffly.

"They think something is wrong with me," she pushed.

Elijah took a step closer, whispering fiercely, "That's not it. At all. Okay?"

She nodded, and he took a step back staring towards the door. "Will you take the pills?"

"Probably not."

Wordlessly, he went to the door, keeping his back to her. His demeanor was oddly determined as he glanced back and left.

*****

Lauren had spent the evening tossing and turning in her uncomfortable bed. When she managed a few minutes of sleep, she'd dreamt of Quinn. It was more than just an uncomfortable dream of her ex-boyfriend. Of course, this was because of his gesture with the pills. Even now, with her missing like she was, it held true that Taylor would still be trying to help her. Her loneliness and longing for her old life was only made worse by the knowledge that Taylor would have been the donor for this batch of pills.

After her talk with Elijah, she felt more trapped than ever. This wasn't an existence where she could travel unless it was on a mission. And by the looks of Barbara, leaving wasn't something she readily got to do. What was she waiting for?

It was still dark outside to her relief as she gathered up her courage. She went to the door, testing the knob that easily twisted within her grip. *When had they stopped locking the door?* She hadn't noticed, since she hadn't tried to escape previously. Maybe they thought she'd gotten used to it here, or maybe someone forgot? At least this part was easy.

She listened to the emptiness in the hallway but knew not to trust it. The nest always had a few Bellators awake when others were not. She pulled the door open, and she peeked out into the empty hallway, listening to hear any presence at the staircase. She couldn't hear anything and slipped out and down the stairs, pausing near the bottom to make sure it was clear.

A warrior was poised at the front door with his back towards her. Unsure of her surroundings fully and needing a hiding spot temporarily, she made the choice to head down the hall towards the training room. There was no exit from the training room or even the room where she sorted the bundled clothes. There was only one other door, and she had no idea where it led.

She grabbed the mystery door's handle and peeked inside, not seeing anyone or anything other than a few racks in the darkness. She stepped inside the pantry, closing the door behind her for a moment to plan out the next move. She searched the racks for any sharp instrument to use in defense. Only bundled fabrics welcomed her fingertips. As she turned to check the other rack, her feet caught, tripping her to the floor in an audible *humph*.

Her fingers reached out into the darkness to move the bundle that she'd tripped over when she recognized what it was. It was a warm, soft bundle that caused her stomach to tighten with further anxiety. She searched the binding until she was able to untie it completely.

The warm bundle made a few adjustments before grabbing at her hands. "Jenny, how'd you find me?"

"I'm not Jenny. Who is she? Where is she?" Lauren asked.

"Who are you?" the frightened girl asked.

"I'm no one. Now where is Jenny being kept?"

The girl stayed silent, only making Lauren worry more.

"I'm leaving. I can't help you or your friend if you don't tell me now," Lauren pushed.

Still the girl remained silent in the dark room. Lauren stood, going to the door to check to see if there was anyone passing by. That's when she felt the gentle tug of her sleeve. The girl was more banged up than Lauren first thought, but with determination, she pointed to the floor. That explained why Lauren had never seen or heard the humans in the nest. Other than that one night...

"How do we get down there?"

Quietly, the girl went to check the hallway before ducking into a small passageway that Lauren had never noticed. They went down a few steps and into an even darker corridor where the girl crouched down to the floor near a trap door. She tugged on the handle with no success. Lauren also gripped the handle tightly, not wanting to think about how hard it would be to force it open. She wasn't sure what she feared more—the noise being loud enough to attract the attention of a warrior and have them all be caught, or not being able to get any of them out at all.

Lauren tugged on the door with Jenny and cringed as it creaked. They paused, checking their surroundings, listening, but no one came down the corridor. They continued to lift the door, but the more it opened, the louder it creaked, freezing Lauren's actions.

"Go get them to come out. I'll hold this open, but we can't move this

47

anymore," Lauren whispered.

The girl nodded, sliding into the open space and into the darkness. The silence dragged on for what felt like minutes. Lauren's eyes flicked between the corridor opening and the opening of the trap door. *What is taking so long?*

Lauren ducked her head inside, noticing that there were only three humans down there. Two were tugging on the restraints to free the last human. "Hey," she whispered. "Come hold this."

The two human girls came back into sight, squeezing out into the corridor with Lauren. "Jenny?" Lauren asked softly.

"Yeah, I can hold this," Jenny replied.

Jenny looked at her friend. "Nancy, help me keep this still."

Lauren went down into the basement area, the smell of musk and staleness hitting her fully with every step, finding the third human tightly bound in restraints. She saw nothing in the room apart from restraints dangling from walls. She needed no more hints as to what the room was made for.

As she approached the young man, she noticed that the more the girls had tugged and the more he had tried to break free, the tighter the ropes had become. She tried to pry some wiggle room with her fingers, but it wasn't going to work. She bent down using her sharp teeth to cut through bits of the rope until he could release one arm. It took a few more bites until he was completely free.

"Nancy, someone's coming," Jenny whispered.

Lauren grabbed the human male, whisking him up into the corridor with the girls. She took them back into the storage room with the bundled fabric. It was a tight squeeze, but it was dark and out of sight. She peeked out into the hallway through a crack, noticing the Bellator who had been guarding the front entrance was now passing by and down toward the corridor. Had they made too much noise?

She held her breath to keep silent, watching him proceed. This might be the only chance they got. She checked the hallway toward the door and saw no one in sight.

"Ready?" Lauren whispered. "Let's go now."

Lauren opened the door only enough for them to slip out. She stayed in front of the humans as they made their way. She could see the shadow of a Bellator at the top of the stairs. She was almost certain he wasn't looking in their direction. She gestured for the escapees to go one at a time out of the front door.

Luckily, Jenny turned the knob without a problem and went out. The other two humans followed her. Yelling began to come from the corridor behind her. It was now or never. Lauren ran out of the front door, taking the extra second to close it quietly.

The night was quiet without even a light breeze to rustle the branches in the trees. She had no idea where the humans had run off to, which was a good thing in her opinion. She didn't want to have any reason for them to remember her other than as the one who helped them. Now she had to help herself. With adrenaline pounding loudly in her ears, she blurred a path into the woods.

The memory of her stumbling upon the nest the night after she became a full Sanguis Bellator sprang to mind. She had been running away from the monster inside, right to the house full of them. Now she was running right back to her safe haven.

It wasn't long until she noticed the cabin in the darkness. Her eyes frantically searched the area in front of her and behind her to make sure she wasn't followed. She couldn't truly be certain either direction was safe, but she needed to get away as fast as she could manage. Any chance of her running from her current location all the way to the campus was a lost cause. She could blur, but not forever. Her legs felt like jelly as she found the hidden key to go inside as she reached the cabin.

Lauren grabbed up the phone with one person in mind. "Taylor?"

"Lauren? Where the hell have you been?"

"I'm sorry. I'm so sorry. Please come get me. As fast as you can," she said hurriedly.

"Where are you?"

"The cabin," she replied in an even lower voice. She carefully checked outside through one of the windows. There was no movement in the shadows that she could tell. "I don't think I was followed."

"I'm on my way," he said. She could hear his movements through the phone line. "Stay on the line with me."

"'Kay." The itchy feeling of being watched refused the ease the tension within her. Deep down, she knew that escape from the Bellator nest was only part of her freedom. Staying away for good was the rest.

# Chapter Five

Time was not on her side, not that the sky would give away what time it truly was. It felt as though an hour had passed as she paced the small building with the cordless phone in her hand. Any noises outside stopped her in her tracks. She'd made sure to keep still and quiet. Maybe it was an animal, maybe it wasn't, but she'd rather not give anything or anyone further reason to investigate the cabin.

"Here," Taylor said through the open line.

She checked outside of the window, noticing his vehicle idling in front of the door with the headlights off. Lauren made sure the coast was clear the best she could before running from the cabin and hopping into Taylor's vehicle. He didn't hesitate to punch the gas pedal with vigor back in the direction he'd come. Her eyes scanned the road behind them while he focused in front.

"Where are we going?" she asked.

"Campus?" Taylor questioned.

"No!" she blurted, panicking. "That'll be their first guess. I need to be *far* away from there."

"Where then?"

"Somewhere I've never been before. I don't want to lead them home," she replied.

Taylor agreed with a nod before handing her his phone. "Call Quinn."

Her fingers worked the phone until it began to ring on speakerphone. Questions blasted her mind with every ring, wondering what her escape could mean since Elijah was so informed about her life. Her habits. Her friends. Would he use the college campus against her? She knew Raeffe would, but with Elijah being closest to her, it would make sense to have him be the one to bring her in. She rolled her eyes not wanting to think of it at all.

"Yeah?" Quinn questioned, half-asleep, his voice raspy over the speakerphone.

"Quinn, it's Taylor," he began.

"I figured that out all on my own," Quinn quipped.

"I got her."

The phone fell silent. Had the call been disconnected? She stared at it and realized the line was still open.

"Hey, Quinn," she said softly.

"I can't believe it. Lauren?"

"Yeah, it's me," she replied.

"Where are you? How'd you get out?" Quinn asked.

"I found a way. Taylor picked me up and we're on our way to nowhere."

"Have you fed?" Quinn asked.

Lauren instinctively wanted to growl back a response. It was like nothing had changed, although she knew it had. "No."

"We're going off the grid for tonight just to make sure no one has followed us," Taylor advised.

"Be careful on campus, okay? Elijah knows it very well," Lauren warned.

"Yeah, I already know."

"Is he there now? Has he already showed up?" Lauren asked, her voice rising with panic.

"No, he isn't here," he said with a dark tone.

"What?"

Quinn sighed over the phone line. "Elijah isn't unknown to us. I knew he was around, but Fallon refused to acknowledge him. Imagine the tension when he showed up to speak with me directly about you."

Lauren's eyes widened in disbelief. *They know about Elijah already? And no one had mentioned this to me. Typical.* She tried to stay focused on the conversation, but her frustration was leaking out. "I'm surprised Fallon hasn't tried taking him out. Especially since she had no qualms about going after me."

"Lauren…" He hesitated on the line. "Elijah's her brother."

Her teeth clenched together, stopping any words from pouring out of her mouth. She had stared at Elijah, knowing deep down that she recognized him from somewhere. His eyes were not exactly like Fallon's, but they were close. Their manner of brushing people off was the same except she saw more in him. Maybe it was because she was being held against her will that she thought she saw that. Maybe he was as ruthless as Fallon, after all. Thinking of him was only making the situation worse.

"He will come to you first, Quinn. He knows the comfort I find on campus," she admitted.

"I'll let Fallon know what to expect. You do what you have to."

"Don't answer any calls that come from my cell phone number. I don't have it with me," she said.

"Keep your phone on you," Taylor advised. "We'll be in touch."

"Sure," Quinn said before hanging up.


After an hour of driving up the highway and a half-hour of driving back roads, a small motel beckoned them with the tiny red vacancy sign lit up. Taylor went into the office while she kept her eyes dutifully on the lookout for anything out of place. Her fear of being followed had lessened after speaking with Quinn. She hadn't realized that the majority of her worries were not focused on herself as much as her vulnerable human companions.

Lauren had always wondered what Fallon had against Bellators from the beginning, but she couldn't have guessed that it would strike so close to home for the girl. Maybe Fallon was using Lauren as a focal point for all of her anger against Bellators because they had changed her brother. She couldn't kill him, but she could avenge him by killing as many others as she could manage. She couldn't even think about the two of them fighting each other.

Fallon was fast, strong and smart when she was determined to fight. Elijah, stalking the campus, would know that, too. Would he actually kill his sister, though?

Taylor shortly emerged from the office with key in hand. He climbed behind the wheel of the car, parking closer to the room around the back of the motel. Handing off the key, he sent Lauren inside first. She checked the area before heading towards the room, slipping inside quickly. She flicked on the lamp on the end table taking in the eggshell-colored walls with framed landscape watercolor paintings. The two full size beds took up most of the room, leaving barely enough room for a dresser with a small TV sitting on the top of it. The bathroom was tiny, but it would do for now.

Taylor came into the room with his duffle bag, kicking the door shut behind him. "I grabbed a few things before I took off."

She watched him unzip the duffle on the bed, tugging it open for her to go through. Her hands pulled out a few shirts, a pair of jeans and undergarments. Her mind couldn't quite catch up to where she stood. So much had happened within a short period of time. All she wanted to do was live in the moment to acknowledge that she was on her own.

"Did I forget something?" he asked.

Lauren shook her head, not concerned about the items within the duffle bag. She had so much more to be concerned about. She glanced up at her best friend who had come to help her. His dark eyes were welcoming as his lower lids were colored a light purple. It felt as though she'd been gone for months as she took in the sight of him.

Taylor stared at her for a moment before wrapping his arms around her in a tight embrace. She closed her eyes, finally being where she had wanted to be. Her mind flooded with things to say, but she did her best to shut it all out. She only wanted to be in the moment with him. Everything else could wait.

*****

Lauren showered, scrubbing off more than that evening's event. Changed into fresh clothes, she finally felt like her old self. Her hair was lifeless after using the motel shampoo and conditioner but they wouldn't be here long. She knew that escaping the nest was the first step; now she had to make the next step in her plan. When she emerged from the bathroom, Taylor's phone began ringing.

Taylor grumbled as he rolled over to answer it. "What is it?"

Lauren sat on the edge of the bed as he put it on speaker.

"They're here on campus," Quinn announced.

"Are they attacking people?" Lauren asked.

"No, which would be a good thing other than the fact that they're hunting for you. It's wise that you didn't come back here."

"How many are there?" she asked.

"Three that I saw coming back from Fallon's. I already let her know. She is on high alert," Quinn admitted.

"You both need to stay low key, all right? This is much bigger than you thought," she said. "Remember when you said that my DNA was different? They know it, too."

Taylor stared at her while she explained that her female transformation had been unique. She made sure to explain Barbara's part in the nest, which dwarfed in importance when Erebus was mentioned.

"King? There's hierarchy?" Quinn asked.

"I don't know much about it, obviously. The only person who could fill me in is Elijah, and I doubt he's speaking to me right now."

"What does that mean?" Taylor asked.

"Elijah was the one who took me the night of the fire. He's been watching over me. Raeffe is his boss, who hates the very mention of my name. He'll make this hard on both of us," she admitted.

"Both of you? Don't tell me that you're worried about Elijah," Quinn stated sternly over the line. "He would kill you if ordered to."

"I know, but—"

"But?!" Quinn interjected. "Are you kidding me?"

"I'd already be dead if it weren't for him. Erebus had already made the order for it to be done. Elijah saved me. I don't doubt that he will do what he needs to, but part of me is hoping there is an alternative."

"What are you thinking? Obviously there is more going on than you're saying," Quinn pushed back.

"I'm a fugitive, Quinn. Unless I can think up some way of staying away from all of the Bellators, I'm good as dead. For now, I'm on the run."

\*\*\*\*\*

Taylor, refreshed from his own shower, began to pack up the duffle bag. She had no idea where they would go next, but only one night in one place seemed like the smart thing to do. There was only one question that hung in the balance.

"Do you want to wait for the sun to set?" he asked.

"Only if you don't have a hoodie."

"Here," he said, handing her one from the duffle bag.

Lauren donned it, allowing the bagginess of it to cover her fully. She tossed her hair into a high messy bun before throwing up the hood that hung down, covering a good portion of her face. It would do for now.

"The city will be better cover with so many people around," Taylor said.

"Are you going to drop me off?"

"Drop you off? Where?" he asked, confused.

"I'm the one they're after, Taylor. You could easily drop me off somewhere safe. They don't know about you, and I don't—"

"No. I'm not going anywhere," he stated firmly. "Except to turn in the motel key."

He grabbed the duffle bag as they both left the room. He unlocked the car, tossing the bag into the backseat. She got into the passenger seat, using his phone to look up the best vacant place to spend the night. She cringed, looking at the prices of some of the hotels. She didn't have her wallet or any form of identification on her. It was safer that way in terms of the Bellators but not in the human world.

Taylor made it back into the vehicle within a few minutes, and off they went towards the highway that would take them to the city.


The sunlight was obscured between the skyscrapers. It seemed like they were all trying to one up each other between height and width. They weren't far from The Dome. She could barely remember the evening they spent together, watching her favorite band, Links & Chains. It felt as though that was a lifetime ago. Back when life was simpler and complicated, all in one.

A familiar hotel brand claimed their attention. Taylor parked in the lot, leaving Lauren in the car to see if there were any vacancies. It wasn't long before he came back for her and the duffle bag. Safely tucked away in a higher-level room, she could finally feel the tension start to release from her muscles. She lay down on the bed after kicking off her shoes, staring at the ceiling.

The room was esthetically more pleasing than the last but still a bland hotel room. Taylor groaned as he lay back on his adjacent bed. She felt her lips lift at the familiar sound. She watched him stretch out until he was comfortable before he turned, noticing her watching. They hadn't spoken a word about what had happened the last time they'd seen each other, and that was fine with her. Her world was already spinning out of control; inserting further heartbreak wasn't something she intended to do.

"I'm starving," he announced as he reached to grab the dine-in menu.

"We can go out. It should be okay now."

"Don't want to risk it," he said. "Plus, I'm pretty tired."

"Too tired for delicious Chinese food?"

He glared in response. "How far is it?"

"It's right across the street. I saw it when you were pulling into the parking lot. Plus, it's not as expensive as whatever you were going to order off the room service menu."

"Eat with me." It wasn't a question.

"Taylor—"

"You haven't fed. I'm not taking no for an answer. You can have a little and then eat dinner with me. Hiding in public," he said. Not waiting for any response from her, he pulled out a pocketknife from his jeans pocket. He carefully cut his finger before walking over to her. "Don't bite me."

Lauren couldn't help that her mouth involuntarily opened at the prospect of tasting his blood again. It was like her body knew the taste and was overriding her mind. His every step toward her dried out her mouth so that every taste bud could be refreshed altogether, wreaking havoc within her. Her eyes zeroed in on his left ring finger that was slowly erupting sweet nectar, just for her.

"Don't bite me," he repeated.

Taylor slowly inched his hand toward her, but it was a lost effort on his part. With a blink of an eye, he was on his back on the floor as she lapped and sucked on his finger with vigor. The taste exploded her past memory into smithereens. The mixture of the iron and sweetness sent a groan past her own lips. Tingles shot through her body as she exhaled from the heady sensation. Her eyes of their own accord found his to share in the pleasure, and then she froze. He appeared more afraid than she'd ever seen him in her presence.

"Taylor, I'm… so sorry!" She pulled back, sitting on her knees as guilt and shame made itself known. She cupped her face in horror of what had happened. She'd lost control at the mere sight of his blood. She'd never had an experience like that before—never so strong. It was intoxicatingly exciting and pleasurable. And that was enough to put her best friend in such a high risk of losing his own life while trying to save hers. Even now, her mouth craved more, her body vigorously pumping adrenaline through her to keep providing what it had wanted all along. The only thing saving them both was her stubbornness.

She started to get up from the floor when his hand grabbed hers. He tugged her back down until they were face to face. His dark chocolate eyes searched hers as his hands cupped her cheeks.

"You're starving yourself little by little. It's not smart," he said. "I'm more than willing to part with a few drops here and there to keep you alive."

Her chest and throat tightened at his words. "I don't want to be the leech in our friendship, Taylor. Literally."

"You're not. You never will be. I'm offering, okay?"

She nodded, still unsure of herself.

"Are you still hungry?" he asked.

"I've had enough. I don't think I could bear another drop."

Taylor disagreed by his expression but didn't push, deciding to tease her instead. "At least you didn't bite me."

"Oh, shut up."

*****

Seated in a cozy booth, Taylor devoured a platter of sesame chicken with white rice. Lauren sat back, allowing him to eat in peace while she scanned the area for any Bellators. It was a huge advantage being able to blend in with

59

other humans. The only disadvantage was she couldn't tell the difference between human and non-human herself. That was enough to keep her interest from focusing too much on her friend.

"You've got to try this," Taylor encouraged loudly, catching her attention. She rolled her eyes. "No, thanks."

"Seriously, this is the best I've had in a long time." He scooped up a small piece of chicken onto his fork. "Please?"

Her reasons for wanting to decline were purely selfish. It would disrupt the residual taste of his blood that she was holding onto. Any admission of her wants would bring them right back to the hotel room. This was the break they needed; what she needed, too. She'd been so cooped up in the nest that being able to move around freely was just as intoxicating as the taste of his blood.

She opened her mouth reluctantly as he forked it inside. The taste was overly sweet from the sauce and the chicken was lost on her. She did her best to smile and compliment his dinner choice. Inside, she wanted to scream. Her concern was real and correct. His flavor was now absent and masked in the sweet sauce that wouldn't leave her tongue.

"Can we go for a walk after you finish?" she asked. "I haven't been outside in a long time."

He nodded an agreement as he finished eating. He paid the bill and held open the door for her as she exited. The sky was a bright purple color from all of the city lights. The stores were still lit up as people hustled and bustled from the chilly air. She peered through the windows of the stores, looking at different clothing lines, perfume and enticing entertainment.

They had walked a few blocks when she noticed a particular man was following them. He wasn't even looking at them, but still he kept a slow pace in the same direction they were moving. She could tell that Taylor hadn't even picked up on it. Instead of waiting for an approach by a potential Bellator, she

60

took a forward step of her own, slipping her hand into Taylor's.

"Thanks for sharing your dinner with me," she said shyly.

"I knew you'd like the sesame chicken."

"Do you know what I'd like more?" she asked as she tugged him closer.

"I can guess." He didn't hesitate, leaning closely enough to capture her face with his hands. He pressed his lips gently against hers once. "But let's wait until we get home."

Lauren nodded, at a loss for words from his actions. She hadn't meant for him to kiss her. It would only start the trouble between them all over again. All she wanted from him was a committed relationship; something he wouldn't offer. She knew that now. It was whether she was willing to accept it or move on. The distracting kiss was enough to bring her back to her own senses.

As they turned to walk down the sidewalk, she glanced in the glass windows for reflective views behind her. The guy in question had disappeared from sight. Her insides shivered knowing that just because she couldn't see Bellators didn't mean that they weren't there. A jewelry store caught her attention as a temporary break.

Lauren went inside, shuffling between patrons towards the back of the store. She gazed at the necklaces on the turning rack to kill time. Taylor stayed quietly by her side, only nodding along when she commented on a particular piece of jewelry. She hadn't needed to say a word to him. It was clear through his behavior that he felt something was off. Maybe he thought it was just her and not the possible threat it could be.

"Want to head back?"

He shrugged indifferently.

"Ice cream?" she asked.

Taylor smirked. "Didn't that get you in trouble the last time?"

"Honestly, I think it was more the jalapeno poppers," she chuckled.

"Come on," she encouraged.

When they emerged from the store, nothing seemed to be out of place. Hand in hand, they ventured to the closest ice cream parlor. She made sure to get a kid size cone to consume as they walked back towards the hotel. Any Bellator that thought she wasn't human would now be hunting elsewhere. Once inside the security of their room, she tossed the rest of the dessert.

"How do you feel?"

"All right, I guess, but I felt fine at first the last time, too," she admitted.

"Can you refrain from jumping me?" he teased.

"I'll see what I can do."

This time he cut the tip of his middle finger. She felt her restraint weakening as once again his blood erupted from the skin. Part of what Taylor had said was true; she had been starving herself to dangerous levels. One thing that caused her further worry was how she responded to *his* blood in particular. When she was at the nest, the blood-filled cups were abhorrent to her.

"Taylor, I…"

"What?"

"I want…" She was losing the restraint she was grasping with all of her might.

"What is it?"

"I want your blood." Her admission was like a swift knife to her soul. Her hands grabbed his awaiting offer without conscious thought. The second the blood touched her tongue, her restraint was gone. She moaned so deeply it barely registered against her ears. The only effort she could afford was to keep from ripping his arm from its socket. It wasn't until she was licking the surface of his finger clean that she felt her composure regain its full strength.

Taylor stared at her in wondrous amazement. "Better?"

"You have no idea," she said. "But we can't keep doing this."

# Chapter Six

Her hazel eyes opened to darkness as she sat up abruptly from the bed. Her eyes couldn't decipher anything around her as her hands trembled with fear. Where was she? The room was too dark to see anything in particular. She got up to look out of the window only to see city streets and cars already speeding down the road. Lauren grabbed her shirt and jeans, throwing them on just as the door swung open.

The sight of Taylor was welcoming and irritating all at once. "Breakfast?"

Lauren plopped back down on the bed, releasing as much tension as she could in the gesture. "No."

"Did I scare you?" he asked, carrying a bag to the bed before kicking off his shoes. "Sorry."

"I didn't say that you did," she replied, annoyed.

"You didn't have to. Want some French toast sticks?"

"I'm not eating today," she groaned, rolling over into the pillows. She couldn't be sure what had set off the nightmare. It could have been the stress finally breaking through her mental walls. How long could she really expect to keep it together? Not only had she been kidnapped, but she had almost been killed. No matter how much bravado she spat at Quinn, she certainly didn't want to die. Not for nothing, anyway.

Taylor ate his breakfast on the end of his bed in silence while she tried to pull herself together. It was only a matter of time before she would have to deal with the Bellators. There was no way she could have Taylor involved. He was strong and smart but nothing compared to what she'd seen a Sanguis Bellator accomplish. He wouldn't stand a chance. And for her own sanity, she needed to put some space between them.

She took her time showering under the hot water to help release the tension. Had she made the right choice to leave the Bellator compound? They were trying to train her, maybe brainwash her into joining in on their missions. It wasn't an existence she could endure for long. But they would have seen her hesitation and possibly taken her out. It was a sobering thought.

She tossed on clothes and came back into the room just as Taylor answered his phone. He was clearly irritable until he broke through the silence.

"You and I both know that that will never happen. I won't let it."

Lauren sat down on the edge of the bed while he conversed. She felt awkward trying not to listen in on his conversation but there was only so much space in the room. Unless she went back into the bathroom...

"I said no," he repeated. His dark eyes focused on her for only a second before he pulled the phone from his ear. "Quinn is trying to get us killed."

"Let me talk to him."

"That's what he wants," he growled.

Lauren missed the cue he was dropping but stuck out her arm for the phone. She put it on speaker to keep Taylor informed, although with his growing anger, it might not get things solved. "It's me. What's up?"

"You'll never guess who is here harassing us about you," Quinn quipped.

"Who?"

"Elijah," he said irritably.

"Is he there now?"

"I told him we didn't know where you were. It would be highly suspect if I handed him the phone now," he said.

"He knows you're lying."

"No shit. And to make it all that much worse, his hanging around has driven Fallon almost over the edge," he said. "She's not sleeping hardly at all, Lauren. She barely eats. And she only thinks about hunting them. We both know how much sleep deprivation can put you at a disadvantage in a fight."

"Find him and call us back. I'll get him to back off of both of you. It'll be okay," she said, hanging up the phone.

"He's one of them. He won't listen to you," Taylor said.

"He will, too. Who do you think helped me out? He left the door open. It was my choice to walk out of it."

"You're not going back," he stated sternly. "Even if we have to leave the country."

Lauren went to sit beside him, leaning against his side. "You're trying to run away with me now?"

"As long as it meant you were safe."

"I know you're worried about me, but it will be okay. We'll figure something out. Besides, I don't have a passport," she admitted, trying to lighten his mood.


Their tender moment was shattered by the sound of the phone going off. She could feel the tension resuming its course through his body. She had to handle this the right way or her promises of this situation getting better would be a total lie. At this rate, she had a little bit of wiggle room speaking with Elijah.

"Hey," she said. "Quinn?"

"Where are you?" Elijah asked menacingly.

"You'll never find me," she said. "Why are you bothering the humans?"

Elijah growled over the line, "My presence here is my own business. However, your freedom is now limited. Erebus put out an all-points bulletin to find you. Alive."

"He wants me for himself, doesn't he?"

"In the worst way imaginable," he admitted.

"Whose side are you on, Elijah?"

"I am loyal to my nest," he said.

"And to your sister?"

Silence greeted her. Maybe he hadn't wanted her to know his connection to Fallon. Well, it was useless trying to hide behind it now.

"Yes," he said shortly.

"Where does that leave me?" she asked.

"The in between," Elijah stated briskly. "I have to get back. Wherever you are, stay hidden."

"Thanks."

"So now what?" Quinn griped in an even sourer mood than earlier.

"I'm working on a plan, but for now I need to lay low," she replied. "How's Mousey doing?"

"He's fine and impatiently awaiting your return. Just like Fallon and I."

"I'm sure she isn't thinking about me."

"This has brought up the one fear she's had for years since Elijah's disappearance. She hates what he is, but I think she'd rather him still be around. Even if she can't accept him."

Lauren sighed heavily into the line. "I understand that more than you'd ever know."

"By the way, I covered for you with your professors."

"You did?"

"Told them you were in an accident that left you unable to attend classes. They understood for the most part. I doctored some papers, so keep that under your hat," he explained. "Your email will have the work in it. You just have to do it and send it back."

"You forged documents for me?"

"Again, keep that to yourself. Although I'm sure *he* heard it," he said.

"Who? Taylor?"

He ignored her response. "Keep me informed on the plan." He hung up with that.

*****

Lauren paced the room as her mind flew through ideas. Her fighting skills were undeveloped and unpracticed. She had to stay out of sight until she could do something. What could she accomplish? What made her different? It wasn't just because of the company she kept. Elijah saw something in her, too. Why else would he not be hunting her?

Her choices of action were thoughtful for the most part. Attacking people and consuming their blood was abhorrent to her, present company aside. Although, she only wanted to taste Taylor. Her focus was on protecting Taylor and keeping him out of any peril. After her reaction to the first taste of him in this room, she was well aware of how intense and dangerous feeding could be.

She stared at him as he watched TV, doing his best to give her the space she needed in cramped quarters. Her mind fluttered back to when she had roomed with him. He'd never bothered caring to give her space; that just wasn't his way. And now he was doing just that? That's when she noticed his flickering glances when he thought she wasn't paying attention.

Lauren couldn't deny all the emotions filling her up when it came to him. The fact that he came without question when she called spoke volumes. Being in love with Taylor was only opening her eyes to what was truly at stake. And it was more than she expected.

"Hey," he said into the phone. "No, not tonight."

"Let me know when, and I'll try to make it," Taylor continued and then paused. "I can't."

He flipped on the basketball game. "Hilary? No. I'm with Lauren." She eyed him warningly at the sound of her name. "She's not doing so good right now."

"Fuck Collin. I don't give a shit what he thinks. Like he'd know what to do with her if she ever gave him the time of day," he flared. "And for the record, we're *friends*."

When Taylor's eyes met with Lauren's, there was no disguising how incorrect the terminology was. He could hear it in his own voice. She certainly could. Her ears felt red hot although she wasn't eavesdropping. Fighting her instinct to push forward the subject instead, she pulled the phone from Taylor's surprised hand.

"Hey, Tony? It's Lauren," she said meekly.

"Oh, hi."

"I'm sorry I borrowed Taylor tonight. I just needed my best friend," she explained.

"Yeah, I get it. That's cool. Have you talked to Hilary?"

"I haven't been able to talk to anyone apart from Taylor," she admitted miserably.

"Oh..."

She handed the phone back to Taylor so that he could end the conversation his own way. She'd helped get the suspicion off of him for the most part. How insane was that? Collin was still trying to work his way into her life. The biggest player on campus who could have any girl but refused to let her off his mind. And here she stay with her best friend, whom she loved and would do anything for, who apparently wouldn't even think about being with her romantically. Friends...

Taylor ended the call shortly afterward, but his mood remained foul. They both knew why; it was only confusing her more, though. Why be agitated that Collin was interested when he wasn't?

"Who's playing?"

He only mumbled a response that she couldn't understand.

"Did you bet on this game?" she asked, feigning interest on the television set. His silence only caused her to keep asking questions that he didn't seem to care for. She stayed away from the important ones that screamed throughout her mind.

"Are you hungry?" she asked to distract him.

"No, are you?" Taylor responded gruffly.

Lauren shook her head, lying through her teeth about the thirst that seemed to never go away in regards to him.

"Sorry," he said just as gruffly.

"Maybe you should go back," she said, hating the words but knowing them to be true anyway.

Taylor looked up at her with a mixture of anger and surprise. "What?"

"You're going to have to go back at some point," she said factually. "I can't keep you on the run with me. That's not fair to you and your life. And I know that one day, *he* will find me."

If she'd blinked, she'd have sworn he knew magic. His arms crushed her to him almost painfully, shoving her back against the wall of the room. She knew deep down to her core that he'd never hurt her purposefully. That thought didn't relieve her worry at the sudden and expressive gesture, though.

"Whether you'll admit it or not, you're pissed at Collin for wanting me so badly. You don't want me, Taylor, but you don't *really* want me with him, either," she admitted.

Taylor began to shout even though she was close enough to hear his heartbeat. "I'm here, aren't I?! You needed me, and I came."

He was missing one of the most important parts, though. This was not about them trying to figure things out. Her world no longer included him, and putting him in it could get them both killed. She knew that. "But don't you see that my future is different now? Love isn't in the cards for me anymore. I'm a Bellator now."

"Not to me," he responded. "Not with me."

"I can't keep feeding on you," she said. "It's weird."

"Believe it or not, it isn't so bad. Just—"

"Don't bite you. I remember," she finished. "It doesn't scare you?"

"Not as much as you fading away does." His lips pinched a couple of times.

"What is it?"

"Nothing," he said. "I'm gonna grab a shower."

His mood was swiftly ranging without a hint of where it would go next. As much appreciation as she felt that he came to get her, she was wondering if this wasn't a mistake of its own. This situation was much more temporary than she first thought.

*****

Lauren stared up at the ceiling, another night of staring until her anxiety receded enough for her to become unconscious. She reached down, scratching her left leg. She examined it in the darkness with her fingers, noting nothing revealing. The wound had looked much worse when she first arrived at the nest. With the help of Bellator remedies, it had eventually healed. What had made it such a big deal? Part of her knew that she would heal eventually. Fallon had stabbed her almost fatally before, and she'd healed almost right away. What was different now?

Barbara had been adamant about her feeding so that she'd heal faster. It was no secret to anyone now that she wasn't feeding, other than her recent activity with Taylor. There had to be something that she was missing. Erebus had asked her why she was different; it wasn't only her who didn't know. What exactly made her different? How?

Taylor was passed out in the bed beside hers with his head tucked beneath the pillow. She checked the clock, revealing it was about one in the morning. It was pretty late, but maybe Quinn would still be awake. She grabbed Taylor's cell phone from the end table and took a trip to the bathroom. The phone rang more than few a few times before it was answered.

"What is it?" he answered crankily.

"Sorry, Quinn," she began. "I know it's late, but I needed to ask you about my DNA."

He muffled a yawn. "What about it?"

"The Bellators knew I was different. It was obvious to them for some reason. Erebus asked me why, like he was trying to get an understanding. You have been trying to figure out *what* makes me different, not why, and I wondered if you had found anything?"

"At one in the morning? No, I haven't," he griped.

Lauren ignored his attitude although she was surprised by it. "If you have any of my life force left to test, can you look into that?"

"What makes you think—"

"Just keep trying. If you need more of my life force, I'll send Taylor to you with it," she advised.

"No, I have some left. Unlike human DNA, your life force doesn't degrade as quickly."

"All right. Sorry for waking you," she said soberly.

"Hey, Lauren... wait," he began. "I will check it out in the morning, okay?"

"Yeah, okay."

"What was it like?" Quinn asked. "With them?"

"It was lonely and uncomfortable."

He stayed silent on the line for a moment. "Can I ask where Elijah falls into this?"

"He was the only reason I got free. Although, I'm sure he is regretting it now," she admitted. "I know he can be scary, but he's watching over Fallon, and that much you can understand. He wouldn't let anything bad happen to her."

Quinn refused to acknowledge the comment. "And you?"

"What about me?"

"Is he protecting you?" he clarified.

"I'm protecting myself, which might be the smartest thing I've done yet in this new existence."

# Chapter Seven

Hours later, she was lying on the bed, still staring at the ceiling with minimal actual sleep. She sat up at the sound of the cell phone going off on the end table. Taylor grumbled from below his blankets as she grabbed it up. Quinn's name flashed across the screen.

"It's me."

"Yes, it is," Quinn stated cryptically. "You're the key."

"The key? To what?"

"Destroying the Bellators," he said quietly into the line. "I did what you said. I didn't think anything would actually happen, but it did! I was checking out your DNA and tripped over my own feet, spilling your life force into other Bellator DNA. The second your DNA came into contact with theirs, it practically caught fire and began to smoke a thick black cloud."

"Wait, wait, wait. Are you sure? I mean, have you tried the same thing with other Bellators' DNA—"

"Yes," Quinn said cutting her off. "It had no effect at all. Just yours did."

"Wow." It was all she could say. It had been just an idea. And that idea certainly wasn't wrapped into it being a weapon. She was a walking, talking weapon that could potentially destroy an entire populace. "What about Erebus? Have you heard about him at all?"

"Not 'til you mentioned him, but I'm looking into it. Still, this is pretty major, Lauren."

"I... I don't know what to say," she admitted.

"Think about this. I've been looking for a cure to turn Bellators back to human. What if the only cure is..."

"Death," she said.


Lauren thought through a few different plans on how to deal with the Bellator situation, but every one of them resulted in sending her right back to the nest. That was the downfall. Did she truly want to go back? Absolutely not. She'd vomited her life force right in the face of Raeffe, and it hadn't affected him at all. It had to be life-force-to-life-force contact. This much she knew now.

She got cleaned up, packing everything used back into the duffle bag. Taylor wasted no time after his shower, filling up the duffle with his belongings before they made their way out of the hotel. She made a pit stop in one of the smaller stores for supplies. Taylor drove out of the city back into the farmlands by the highway.

While he drove, she used the few supplies she bought. Darkening the eyeliner around her eye and adding more mascara to her lashes, she heard him sigh. "What?"

"I don't like this plan," he said.

"It's the best option right now. They don't know the real me."

"Will it matter?" he asked.

"Of course, it will. Erebus wants to kill me in front of everyone. It will make him look more important."

"Again, I don't like this plan," he complained.

"As long as there are no extra surprises, I should be okay."

She knew the only real chance she had was her honesty. They'd already seen what that looked like in her previous state. Now she had to keep it going. There was only one issue with her plan. Elijah.

"When you were away, I kept having these…" Taylor said, pulling her out of her thoughts, "dreams of you."

"What kind of dreams?"

"There's this room decorated like from medieval times. It's filled with a bunch of people in it, lined up and staring like they've been waiting for me. There's a creepy guy with cold blue eyes who looks like he can see right into my mind," Taylor said. He described the questions and then the presentation of the pear of punishment before being grabbed up. "I knew that I was in a dream, but couldn't do a damn thing about it. It pissed me off. I couldn't sleep the rest of the night. I kept wondering where you were, if you'd come back, if I'd ever see you again."

Lauren grit her teeth in silent horrification. He saw her. He saw that! Of all the things he could have dreamt, this was the worst possibility. There was no question that she'd have to deny any knowledge of it. It was awful enough knowing that he had seen what she'd gone through, but his peace of mind was all she could think of. He didn't need to know it was true.

She couldn't begin to start wondering how he managed to see it. If she could lessen the likelihood of his belief in it, then that would help. Later, she could ask Quinn about it. Unless he was having visions of her activities, too. Fudge-o-lees!

"Don't worry about your dreams. Reality is enough trouble," she said.

His vehicle pulled into the parking lot as the stars twinkled in the night sky. He jumped out, going into the slate-colored dorm building that she'd resided in with him. Part of her wanted to go along, too. Being back on campus was the one thing she wanted the most. She quickly typed a text to let Quinn know their status.

*5 mins and gone.*

*Be there in 2,* Quinn replied.

Lauren bundled up, tucking her hair into her hoodie as she covered her head. It was only a minute when she noticed Taylor come back with her recognizable overnight bag. She climbed out of his car, tugging along the duffle bag.

"Switch out your stuff, and I'll load it up," he said.

She made quick work changing out the clothes she wanted to keep and accessories he had brought initially to put into the overnight bag he brought out of the dorm. He started her car, allowing the heat to warm it up as two figures appeared in the darkness. Her breath slowed at the approach until they reached the front of the car.

"Thought it best if you took this with you," Quinn advised, handing her a small, thin box.

"What is it?" Lauren inquired.

"Protection," Quinn stated.

"Thanks. Did you find anything about *him*?" Lauren asked.

"Not really," he admitted.

"I'll do extra research to find out more," Fallon said.

Taylor tossed the last of her luggage into the backseat of her car. His dark eyes weren't lost on her, nor was the concern within them. She took in Quinn and Fallon, the two people whom she had no idea would still be willing to help her after turning into a Sanguis Bellator. Her heart swelled, causing an uncomfortable ache within her chest. Emotions were a human characteristic that she'd been fighting since the day she'd been attacked.

"Thanks for everything," Lauren said to both of them. "I should go."

"Be careful," Quinn advised.

"Give them hell," Fallon stated.

Lauren nodded an agreement before they headed back towards campus. She turned towards the driver's side door. Taylor came to her side wordlessly, searching her face like he had done a thousand times before.

"I love you," Lauren confessed. "I'm sorry, but I do. I'm in love with you, and I need you to know. I might not get another chance—"

Taylor brought his lips to hers roughly, stopping any further admissions. He kissed her deeply as she poured her aching heart into the gesture. This could be the last time she ever saw him. At least he knew now how she really felt. That he was loved, even if only by a monster like her. She was alive with him, and if he died, so did she.

"The cabin will have everything you need, okay? I'll keep it stocked up for you."

"They won't let me leave again," she said.

"You're not like them. You'll find a way, Lauren." He embraced her tightly. "I'll be here."

Lauren drove away from the campus with Taylor and her heart in her rearview. Fallon had every right to be as angry as she was, and it made perfect sense now in hindsight. Lauren knew what she had to do, but it didn't make it any easier. She was going to have to turn away from her humanity to survive this. After all, surviving was the number one plan.

# Chapter Eight

As she drove down the all too familiar road towards the nest, her skin began to crawl. Her emotions had been running high since her heart-felt admission to Taylor. He hadn't said "I love you" in return, and she knew that he wouldn't. His feelings were a deep well that the small amount of time they'd spent together wouldn't have been able to fill. And even now, she couldn't put her heart into looking deeper.

The sleek two-story building with the severely shaped roof came into view. It was time to face the reality of what she'd done and accept the side of her that she hated the most. She pulled in beside the building, doing a quick job of fixing her makeup in the mirror. With a deep breath and a great dose of courage, she got out of the vehicle and went to the door, knocking on it.

Barbara opened the door with a shocked expression. "Please come in."

"Thank you, Barbara. I'd like to speak with Erebus if he is awake," Lauren requested.

Raeffe stood merely a few feet away, his normally lethal expression halted by the shock of her reappearance, as well. She smirked in response. "My bags are in the car."

"I'll go check to see if the king is free," Barbara stated.

Lauren pulled back her hood, allowing her mind to focus on each task at hand. Two Bellators followed Barbara back to the entrance where Lauren waited. She didn't need any more confirmation than that. Lauren nodded, accepting her fate as it would be handed to her. Barbara stepped aside as Elijah came down the stairs.

"Here," Lauren said, handing her car key to Elijah. "My bags are in the backseat."

Barbara appeared flustered at her sudden reappearance. Clearly it was unexpected. "Are you hungry?"

"No, thanks. I just ate." It took Lauren a breath to wonder if that was the right answer or not. It was honest, and that would have to do for now.

"Raeffe, please escort her," Barbara said.

Lauren followed his lead down the hallway as Elijah came back inside with her bags. Part of her wasn't sure if she wanted an audience for Erebus or not. Better she come back willingly than as a thief caught red-handed. She had a part to play in this Bellator power play as Elijah had his. And as she entered the room, seeing Erebus sitting on his love seat, staring at her with admiration and bloodlust, she questioned her own intentions regarding whether or not she was truly ready to die.

"Dearest Lauren, how kind of you to deliver yourself to me," he greeted.

"Good evening, King Erebus. It is calming to be back."

"Calming?" he questioned with a cold stare. "I highly doubt that."

Raeffe stood by Erebus' left side. "Where did you go?"

Lauren took in a deep breath that curved her lips into a predatory smile. "Life is what you make it, and I'd yet to understand what that meant. I travelled through towns and city lights that twinkled. I breathed fresh air, tasted forbidden fruit and over-stimulated most of my senses." She ran her fingers through her hair at the thought of the freedom she'd felt while with Taylor. "I hadn't expected to want more. That there was even more to be offered outside of these walls."

Erebus' stare hadn't changed intensity although he was now leaning forward in his seat, as if her words had taken him along for the ride in the outside world. "And what, might I ask, were you not offered here?"

The curl to her lip refused to reside. "Freedom of choice... to eat what I like."

"You have cravings for specifics?" His question came across as his eyes came to life.

Lauren nodded, pretending to hide her devious smile. "I prefer something with a little kick in it."

Raeffe stared at her like she'd just put a spell upon him.

"I see," Erebus said. "Everyone out. Now."

She watched the entire room clear out. Even Raeffe left, albeit dubiously. She suspected he was wondering the same as she was. What was Erebus up to? Certainly he wouldn't kill her; he'd prefer the show of power. This much she was sure of.

To her surprise, Erebus stood up from his cushioned sitting area. His height was easily over six feet as he circled her. She'd be a fool to think he was merely perusing her fresh appearance. With her head held high with feigned confidence, she broke the silence. "What is your purpose?"

"To rule the world," he replied cockily. "Nothing to worry your pretty little head about."

"You think I'm pretty?" she asked, ignoring his condescending tone that went along with his answer.

Erebus smirked, not bothering to respond. "Actions have consequences. You were already on probation when you arrived."

Lauren heard the stern tone allowing it to pass through her. She had wants and needs of her own. Her predatory smile crept upon her face as she carefully and sensually batted her eyes at him. Her temper wasn't going to solve anything today. She needed a softer touch. "I understand power plays, and that is none of my concern. You can punish me if you want, although my level of threat is pretty minuscule," she said, tucking her hair behind her ears. "Actions have consequences, and it was a tasty one."

His interest waned as she spoke, and he returned to his love seat, deciding to sit back down.

She walked up to him, kneeling to keep his head higher than hers. "It was like tasting the sun," she continued. "It was so hot as it erupted onto my tongue, sliding down my throat. Every taste bud imploded, singeing me to the core. I never knew what a pleasure feeding could be."

Erebus nodded, keeping his pale eyes upon her. "You're young. You have a lot to learn."

"Like that?"

"Yes and more," he stated.

Lauren allowed the memory of feeding from Taylor to seep through her. A gentle shiver shook her frame and she used it to her best advantage. "Do all Bellators feel this way?" she asked innocently.

Erebus took in her exuberance and sighed. Had she crossed a line? Was he angry? "You're not to leave the nest again. Especially without proper supervision."

She nodded with hopeful eyes.

"Training will resume as before," he responded, dismissing her.

Lauren nodded, getting up to leave.

He cleared his throat. "And I'll speak with Barbara about your preference. Blood is plentiful and available."

\*\*\*\*\*

Lauren arrived back in her old sleeping quarters with less enthusiasm. The bed would still be uncomfortable, there would be no stimulation in the least to keep her occupied and no contact with the outside world. Returning to the Bellator life was already boring her. Her bags were sitting next to the bed; she figured they had already been searched.

She decorated the room with the few pieces of home that Taylor had thought to toss in. It brightened the bland room, making it a less uncomfortable setting. If she were going to stay here, she would have to make it livable. With her bag unpacked and a spruce of life added, she relaxed upon the bed.

A knock sounded before she heard the door unlock. Elijah entered with a bewildered stare. The change of scene was hardly worth his intense scrutiny, but she was a different matter entirely.

"You fed."

It wasn't a question. The light in her eyes was a dead giveaway, not to mention her emotional stability. He hadn't questioned her over the phone although she wasn't announcing it in mixed company. She had forgotten that he was linked to both of her worlds.

"Are you concerned or happy? Your expressions all look the same," she said.

Silence welcomed her. "Pissed, then, it is. Believe it or not, I did think of you."

Elijah glared as he came close enough for her to feel his breath upon her face. Anger was clearly winning over his facial expression and her memory flashed back to when she had fought with Taylor. Her emotional range was limited between anger and passion. Such a thin line between both. It was part of the makeup of who she was. Elijah was nothing like her, but he was not like the others, either.

She stepped forward, wrapping her arms around Elijah's waist in an embrace. She kept her strength at a minimum, unsure of how he would respond. She closed her eyes, not wanting to see his anger but to give him the space to get over it. Was he glad to see her back in one piece? Wasn't he expecting the worst?

"I'm glad to see you, too," she sighed.

His stance relaxed, although he kept his arms to himself. She couldn't be sure if he wanted her to let go or not. Part of her ached to help bring Elijah back into Fallon's life. Monster or not, Fallon loved her brother, which explained why she was so upset about him being changed. There needed to be a way for them to resolve their differences. Fallon dealt with Lauren; certainly she could accept her own brother, too.

Lauren released his form unwillingly. "Erebus sees something in me," she whispered.

"It's not just one thing," Elijah whispered.

"What's that mean?"

"Not many female Bellators are left. A handful maybe. You, though, you pique his interest. Can you not see that?"

She knew she was different, but that concept was at the bottom of the list. "I'm also strange."

Elijah smirked without humor. "He likes a challenge."

She rolled her eyes. "I'm spoken for."

His eyebrows rose with surprise. "Already?"

"Well... Mostly spoken for."

"Who?" he questioned.

"Don't worry about it. You don't know him."

"A Bellator?" he whispered. "A human? You really are trying to get yourself killed."

"I wouldn't expect you to understand," she stated, turning away from him. It was hard enough trying to deal with being back in the nest. She didn't need her love life to be part of his concern. Or anyone's, for that matter.

"Of course, I get it. The problem is you have to stop clinging to the past. It's blinding you to what danger lies ahead," Elijah explained. "You fed on *him*, didn't you?"

She refused to look him in the eye. It was no business of his who she fed on. This conversation was out of the question.

Elijah faced her, tugging her roughly by the arm. "Look, you have to forget your human memories of love and affection. No one here will ever care for you like that. It's all about how they can use you for their own selfish success and increase their standing in the nest. The fact that you haven't been hit on at all yet is even worse. That means someone with real pull has their eye on you, and everyone else knows to back off. I can't help you if you're going to act like an emotional and stubborn human."

"How could you possibly help me? They're not going to let me go now," she said, pissed.

"You do have to feed."

"I'm not bringing him here to be slaughtered," she whispered fiercely.

"Then we'll have to find another way. Erebus would be opposed to any Bellator starving inside a nest."

*****

Training resumed where she'd left it. Unfortunately, that meant she was still getting the basic moves down in a rhythmic motion that was under appreciated. She was only glad that she managed to have some time to practice with Elijah, too. He was much less harsh than the others, although he was stern about the training. She understood the fancy footwork was important but so was being different. If every army did the exact same thing all the time, the opposition would pick up on that easily enough.

She watched the Bellators switch shifts between missions that were never spoken of. Not to her, anyway. She wondered if one day they would put her to work like that. Whatever missions they were, they were very important to the entire nest. Raeffe steered clear of her for the most part. And there were no inquiries about her interest in food. Erebus said he'd talk to Barbara about it; maybe them shutting her out was payback for her leaving.

The room was beginning to close in upon her even with the extra time she spent training or distributing clothes to the warriors. Her tinted view from her room only hinted at what the outside world had to offer. She even missed the chance to sit in the backseat of the car, watching the landscape pass by her. Anything was better than this.

Lauren had just finished up her training downstairs when she came back to the room where a message awaited. She unfolded it and read it to herself.

*"You may seek to fill your thirst this evening. Raeffe will escort you."* - King Erebus

Feeding with Raeffe around would never happen. She couldn't ever bring him near Taylor. And whatever type of feeding the other warriors were used to, she had no idea. She quickly scribbled a decline of the offering and slid it beneath the door to be retrieved by a passing warrior. She'd rather starve to death.

*****

She was peering out of her tinted window when the door opened. To her surprise, Elijah was holding something familiar in his hand. His expression was a bit stiffer than usual; she attributed that to having to deal with her friends. This was to keep her sane and alive after all.

"I've never thought of myself as a blood mule until now," he complained, handing over the bottle of blood-filled capsules. Lauren chuckled softly to lighten his mood. She opened the bottle, taking two of them straight away. "How long will this last you?"

She shrugged, unsure. "When we notice that I'm struggling again, I guess. It's not like I need a certain amount a day. How often do you feed?"

"Barbara keeps us fed every week. Some need more than others. It's an age thing," he explained.

"Age?"

"The older the warrior, the more they must feed. Missions are dangerous, but after a long time the memories and knowledge of what we have done start to cloak us. There's no way to shake it, but feeding seems to keep it at bay until..."

86

"Until...?" she asked.

Elijah shook his head soberly. "The eldest warrior lived to seventy-six before his memories became too much. He went insane. Erebus had to personally come take care of the situation."

Lauren stared with wide eyes. "How old is Erebus?"

"Infinite. He has been working to try to help us all live as long as he has. He doesn't want to be alone anymore," he said.

Even she could see emotion behind that statement. No wonder the Bellators were so quick to try to execute her if they realized her life force could end them. The fear of their own mortality was strong in the nests, especially with Erebus around. He truly didn't want to end her life; she was rarer than she could even fathom. Lauren wrapped her arms around his waist in a hug. It was a horrible future for anyone to think about, the trauma to their soul and psyche, let alone take it in personally. His stance relaxed allowing her to embrace him tighter.

"It'll be okay," she said. Her back warmed as his arms wrapped around her in return. She glanced up at him, willing her positive energy to come across her features. "We will be okay."

Elijah nodded in response as they made a silent promise to themselves.

The door opened quickly, sounding loudly. It was too late for them to react and separate from their embrace. Barbara and Raeffe stood with surprised and disapproving looks. Elijah removed himself effectively from Lauren, stepping back into his usual stance.

"Mission," was all Raeffe said. Elijah left the room briskly with Raeffe following his trail.

"What were you trying to pull?" Barbara asked, not hiding her disapproval.

"Nothing," Lauren replied, shrugging it off and walking back towards the window.

"That didn't look like nothing. There are rules here in the nest about distracting and consorting with warriors. They are busy and don't need distractions of any kind," Barbara pushed.

Lauren glared at her, not bothering to tame her words. "Sure, I just unlocked the door myself and dragged him in here. He *wanted* to be here."

Barbara shook her head in disgust before leaving the room and locking the door.

*****

It wasn't until late into the evening, when Lauren had already been fast asleep, before Elijah snuck into her room. She sat up with a start only to find him with a shushing finger to his lips.

"They think we're lovers," Lauren whispered to him. "How do we fix this?"

"There's only one way to break free from this nest," Elijah advised.

"What do I have to do?" she asked.

"Nexus eternum. It's Bellator law that cannot be undone that allows a couple to travel freely from nest to nest."

The words began to come together in her mind. *A couple?* Her eyes widened. "Like marriage?"

"Yes."

She was speechless. Even her mind couldn't come up with a single thought. Marriage was something she hadn't thought hardly enough about in terms of her own future. There was so much more to consider. When would she finish getting her degree? Would she be able to find a job once she graduated? Would her parents allow her to live with them until she could afford a place of her own? Marriage wasn't even on the table.

"Marriage and freedom don't exactly go hand in hand," she said slowly.

"Not in the human world, but it does in ours. You wouldn't need an escort to feed or be stuck in this room all the time. We could leave, Lauren."

"I—I don't know what to say."

Elijah moved in closely with his volume low enough to be nearly imperceptible. "Say yes," he beseeched her before leaving her alone with her thoughts.

# Chapter Nine

Lauren practiced her training in her room, allowing her annoyance with Fallon to fuel her to push to perfection. The more she attempted to tone down her hip movement, the more off balance she became. She added her arms to help before she finished for the night. In the sanctuary of the room, she trained her upper strength with push-ups until she could manage at least ten without wanting to break down into tears or make her so furious that she spoke aloud. It was all for a good cause. At least this way she would be stronger physically. That would help build up the confidence she needed to hide the human vulnerability she was still dealing with.

*****

Her arms were still trembling with the effort put into her training, but it was worth it. The training warrior hadn't seemed as horribly disappointed in her as last time. The barrage of negativity seemed endless when it came to being around the other Bellators. She was glad to at least get cleaned up in the shower.

That relief came to a stuttering halt as she passed by the familiar corridor that once held Jenny and Nancy. She wondered if the humans had managed to get home safely. There was no real reason why she was even thinking of the girls or why she was headed towards the door except for morbid curiosity. The familiar weight of the door made her shiver as she tugged it open enough to slip inside.

She was prepared for the darkness, as she glanced around not noticing much right away. The sound of clinks was what really caught her attention then. She found a warm, solid body with her fingertips, almost exactly like how she'd found the other girls. In the human's mouth was a gag and over their eyes was a blindfold. Her touch only seemed to scare them more.

"Shhh, it's okay. I won't hurt you," she whispered as she removed the blindfold.

Her hands shook as his eyes revealed his true identity. She couldn't breathe but was glad that she hadn't removed his gag first. The shock on Collin's face lasted only a moment before he whimpered for her to help release him. Part of her wanted to know how he'd found himself prisoner in the basement of the nest but knew she would never be able to get over it. She tugged the gag down covering his mouth before she tried to speak first.

"I'm going to try to get you out," she said.

"I can't believe this is where you've been!" he said, panic tingeing his voice.

Lauren tried to get her hands around the knotted ropes until she realized that heavy chains reinforced them. There was no way to get him free by biting through the ropes. Her heart sank, knowing that she'd have to leave him there temporarily. Elijah might help her if she asked him.

"Collin, I need you to be calm, okay?"

"Calm? Do you know what they did?" he asked, not bothering to give her time to answer. "I was at my car, minding my own business. And this guy walks by name-dropping you. It was so weird, but I hadn't seen you in weeks, and he said you wanted to see me."

"Oh, no… no, no, no."

"Next thing I know, I'm chained down here," he said, now getting a bit angry.

"I'm so sorry. I will get you out. I promise to do all that I can," she said before replacing the gag and blindfold against his protests.

Lauren headed straight for the heavily guarded throne room.

"I must speak with King Erebus."

"He is in a meeting. I will make sure he summons you when available," the warrior responded.

"Please, this is very important," she begged.

The warrior leveled her with a stare that would have made the old Lauren pee her pants. It had to be good luck that just at that moment Elijah walked out of the room. *I gotta do what I gotta do.*

"Elijah, may I speak with you?" she asked as formally and respectfully as she could manage.

He turned, giving her his formal stance before nodding towards the end of the hall to give them a modicum of privacy.

"Why aren't you back in your room?"

"I got distracted by a familiar face," she said, quickly explaining in a harsh whisper who she found. "I know that I'm not supposed to care, however, if he goes missing and everyone on campus knows that he has been obsessing over me, I'm going to be the main focus of attention. That isn't going to help keep the Bellator life a secret."

"I will speak to Erebus about it. You will only come across as a human sympathizer," he said, heading back into the throne room.

Lauren paced the hallway, making no secret of her intention to see Erebus. It wasn't until two Bellators were dragging Collin down the hall and into the throne room that her fears rose to new heights. The guards wouldn't let her into the room until Erebus had given permission. She was surprised when the word finally came, but she went right in.

She knew she had to hide her feelings of fear inside, but the sight of Collin in the hands of Raeffe only caused her concern to deepen. She blinked a few times, trying to keep the blank look upon her face as she approached King Erebus with Elijah standing opposite Raeffe.

"Ah, here she is," Erebus welcomed.

Elijah turned towards her with an irritable expression that only she could

92

see. He certainly wasn't helping her cause, of that much she was sure. Her focus stayed on Erebus from then on. She couldn't trust herself not to look at Collin without giving herself away. And she knew she couldn't look at Raeffe without wanting to rip his head off more than usual. He was messing with the wrong person.

"You were expecting me?" Lauren asked, cautiously hopeful.

Erebus' pale blue eyes leveled her with a don't-play-with-me glance. "Of course, I was."

Lauren blinked up at him with her predatory smile as she slowly approached. "I wanted to discuss the offer you made in the note that was left in my room."

His expression gave nothing away as he continued to push her non-verbally. She went right up to him before kneeling at his feet. She dared not look at anyone apart from Erebus.

"There is nothing to discuss," he said, dismissing her concern. "He will take you, today if you're ready."

"He understands specifics?" she asked.

Erebus eyed her dubiously. "He understands instruction from his king."

Lauren allowed the hope on her face to slip into a polite, but clearly disappointed facade. Her eyes dropped to his feet as she began to get up. It was then that she took in the sight of Collin in Raeffe's hands.

The change in her stance made it clear the shock she experienced seeing a human she knew.

"Timing is everything, isn't it?" Erebus questioned. "Your concern may not be needed now. You two clearly know each other."

Lauren nodded, glad to see that Collin was still blindfolded. "We had a class together."

"It must've been more than that," Raeffe laughed darkly. "He is always talking about you. Even after you left campus."

The way Raeffe said it made it clear that she couldn't deny her friendship with Collin even as minimal as it was. She mirrored his dark laugh. "It seems he has found me, after all. I only hope his friends don't go asking about his disappearance."

"Humans go missing all the time. They will forget. They always do with time."

"The campus is still wondering where I am. They'll suspect he is with me, dead or alive," she said. "Good way to endanger the Bellator way of existence."

"Endangered by who? Humans are weak," Raeffe stated.

"I haven't been in hiding this entire time. I went to the city and the farmlands. Humans will scour for him. And worse, you'll have to be even more cautious when on missions. Humans are weak, but not when it comes to imagination and legends."

"Lauren," Elijah warned. "What is to be done?"

Her eyes flared at him, willing her mouth to not spout off. "Is the choice mine?"

"Of course, it isn't," Erebus replied.

"Dinner is ready," Raeffe stated, shoving Collin to the floor.

"Wait," she said, taking a step towards him.

Raeffe grabbed a handful of Collin's hair, making a quick but forceful snap backwards with his hands. Collin's body fell to the floor in a heap. Lauren froze in utter shock. Slowly, the anger began to form on her face. She couldn't hide it. She couldn't stop it. Her eyes lifted directly at Raeffe who appeared almost giddy.

"Thanks for proving my point," she said before turning back towards Erebus. "He doesn't understand my needs. If he did, he wouldn't have killed one of my favorite humans to feed on."

"Feed on?" Raeffe asked surprised.

Erebus became deathly silent as he stared at her. "What have you been up to?"

She glanced at Elijah who looked horrified right back at her. "What? What's wrong?"

"We do not feed delicately on humans, Lauren," Elijah said with faux seriousness.

"We drink them dry, always," Raeffe said.

"But there was a girl—she was a freshman who was attacked. She survived," Lauren stated.

"She survived the trip to the hospital."

Elijah turned to Erebus, blocking her from sight. "Lauren needs guidance and training. Clearly, she is making it up as she goes along. Please allow me to show her the ropes."

Erebus stood from his love seat. "Raeffe will see to her needs and training."

Lauren felt the anger seep back in, taking over the surprise. "I haven't fed since being back. Maybe that's the plan, after all..."

Silence welcomed her response as she left the room.


There was nothing more she wanted than to end Raeffe's existence. It was a promise that she would keep even if it meant the end of her own life. She could see now how close he and Erebus were. And how she underestimated how clever Raeffe could be. That was the first and last time.

*****

Lauren had so many emotions ricocheting through her as she blurred from one side of the room to the other. She couldn't even dry sob to herself. Her anger had hit a new level by the time Elijah came through the door.

Anything he was prepared to say was halted by the look she gave him.

"I want him dead."

Elijah put his hands up. "Don't start—"

"He started it the second he put his hands on Collin. He brought him here. Here!"

Elijah tried to corner her but she only blurred away in anger. She made three circuits of the room before she slowed down enough to be seen. "Careful now. You said it yourself, you haven't fed. Don't waste your energy."

"I'm not going to feed until *he* is gone," she said. "Erebus can wait another few decades for another female Bellator."

"Stop this!" he demanded. "You can be pissed at Raeffe all you want. But don't you speak in vain of our king."

Lauren looked past Elijah out of the window. "Collin's dead because of *me*."

"Did you feed on Collin?"

Lauren shook her head. "He was a great athlete, an even better friend, and he wanted me. I shut him down and out. Multiple times. How could this happen?"

"It is part of who you are. Collin wasn't the only one affected and drawn to you, and you know that."

"What?"

"Have *you* not been paying attention? You have a list of *human* friends, who risk their lives to help *you* all the time. One specific human who would like to do nothing more than to end your life and yet here you are. It's part of the new you that was born the night you were—"

"Attacked," she said, cutting him off.

Elijah ignored her. "There is more to the female Bellator than what you know. You inspire, captivate, energize and elude every creature you meet.

There was no stopping Collin from becoming addicted to your presence once you showed him even the slightest bit of interest."

"That's ridiculous. I'm not addictive."

"Then why am I here, helping you? Making sure that you're all right after seeing a friend killed," he said plainly. "Bellators kill often, whether they know the human or not. It's an everyday occurrence. Something you need to get used to."

"All lives matter, Elijah. Not just ours." Elijah headed for the door as she spoke up. "Wait, please."

"What?" he said, turning to face her.

"So what does my future look like? Trapped in a nest for fear of leaving and looking at a guy? Are Bellators not as easily affected?"

"Barbara is not trapped here. She stays because it is safe for us. Humans draw attention, and as they become addicted, they're less careful about expressing who and what they want," he explained.

"But I'm trapped here."

"Yes, because you're untrained, volatile and bringing unneeded attention on yourself," he said. "You were practically sitting on Erebus' lap down there. What was with that?"

"Jealous?" Lauren stated sarcastically.

Elijah glared with a don't-even-kid-yourself look.

"What? You're getting addicted to me, too. Are you not?"

"I didn't tell you that to use it against me," he said, grabbing for the door handle.

Lauren placed her hand on the door. "I'm sorry. I don't know why I react that way around him. It keeps happening whenever I'm around him. Like this part of me wants to gain his approval but push his buttons at the same time."

"You were flirting with the king."

"Ugh! Don't say that."

"Bellators are not as easily led as humans are. I don't hate being near you, which is different. Bellators don't particularly like being around each other. Notice all the solo missions."

"Were you avoiding me?" she asked.

Elijah nodded. "You were so broken and pathetic. It took time to understand why I was even paying attention to you."

"And now?"

"You're not so broken anymore. You will get through this."

She sighed. "I didn't realize I was feeding wrong."

Elijah shook his head. "Just pill intake?"

"Ummm…" She looked at the floor, somewhat embarrassed. "Sometimes from a self-inflicted wound."

Elijah stared at her like she had spoken another language. "You need a full body to keep going. How are you even standing?"

"I don't *need* to feed, Elijah. I just get a little emotional from time to time."

"You can't keep feeding on *him*."

"That's not giving mixed signals," Lauren replied sarcastically.

"Do you plan on turning him?"

"No," she said.

"Look, I get it. You and he have history, but you're different now."

"We both know that. This really isn't up for discussion."

"You wanted to be trained. Well, first lesson is don't feed on who you don't plan on turning. I'm honestly surprised he's restrained enough to not come looking for you now."

"He's not like that," she said, knowing that she was the one clinging to Taylor rather than the other way around.

"Here," he said, handing her cell phone back. "Keep the ringer off."

*****

Lauren gripped the phone tightly between her fingers as it rang a few times.

"Hey, you got your phone back," Taylor answered, surprised.

"Yeah. I have some things to take care of. It's not like I can go out."

"How bad was it?" he asked.

"It… was very weird. I'm not sure if Erebus wants to kill me or parade me around like a puppet."

"Power play?"

"It's either that or he likes the idea of being seen as merciful. It's not like I'm a real threat."

"Do you know long you have to stay?" he asked.

Lauren sighed. "No. A while, I'm sure."

"Tony is supposed to be putting something together," he mumbled. "No way you could escape tonight?"

"If there was a way, I'd already be out. Unfortunately, it won't be as easy as last time."

Her worries of Taylor only seemed to grow as thoughts of Elijah entered her mind. Certainly, Taylor wasn't addicted to her. He showed no sign of it apart from his concern for her safety. That was nothing new; even when she was human, he had been protective. Ever since her childhood bee attack, he had made a point to stick close by.

Being around him was something that felt so natural, so normal, even after her transformation. Elijah just didn't understand their relationship or the fact that she was pushing for more from him. But his concern was based on experiences with other female Bellators. She couldn't be that different.

"Do you love me?" she blurted out.

"Lauren—"

"I need to know before I possibly ruin the rest of my existence. Is there even the smallest chance that you feel something for me?" she asked, caught between sudden desperation and fear.

"This isn't really a good time."

"Elijah has proposed marriage to me," she admitted.

"What?" His voice was low and lethal. "What the fuck are you talking about?"

"The only way to get away from this nest and Erebus permanently is to be wed by Bellator law. Elijah proposed freedom for us both."

"That's not freedom, Lauren!"

Lauren agreed completely. The entire situation was bullshit, but Erebus was much more dangerous than she expected. And worse, if she couldn't get from under his thumb with Elijah, they both would fade away. Raeffe was much more clever than she gave him credit for, and she could easily see him going after Fallon or Taylor should he know what they meant to Elijah and her.

The silence was heavy on the line as the only sound she could hear was Taylor's breath. What was she expecting him to say? She'd just dropped this entire situation on his lap after leaving with an unspoken promise to keep herself safe and find a way back to him. Neither of them were ready for the seriousness of this situation.

"I'm not safe to be around anymore. Not because of the Bellators, and not because of my thirst."

"What are you saying? You're taking off?" he asked angrily.

"Taylor, Collin is dead because of me. He couldn't let me go, couldn't stop trying to get closer until someone else got their hands on him to retaliate against me because of my defiance. It's my fault; I know that. I won't let that happen to anyone else that I care about."

"Collin," he said in shock.

"I have more power than I realized. More than Quinn could imagine. I have to take control of my existence, and that leaves minimal options."

"And Elijah is the only way," he said angrily. "That sounds like control. Control over you."

"Taylor, no, it's not like that. I told you—"

"He proposed to you. That was never an option before," he seethed.

"I already told *you* how I feel. This proposition doesn't change anything except for my ability to leave the nest. Believe in me, Taylor."

His breath became heavy on the line. "Do what you have to do to survive."

Lauren closed her eyes, waiting for him to say the words. *Just say the words, Taylor.* All she heard was the line go dead.

# Chapter Ten

She sat there in a daze distributing clothes to the Bellators. Barbara made no qualms about her quiet state. It was almost like she was in a glass box with two holes for her hands to continue working. There was so much at stake. Her freedom was number one on her list. But she knew absolutely nothing about committing to another Bellator. It's not like there were books on it.

When Elijah walked into the room, his expression remained neutral. It was so easy for him to hide within himself. It was something she'd have to learn and quickly. Especially when it came to committing herself to him.

He was a great warrior who was respected within the nest. Yet for some reason, he wanted to leave this place where he'd made a home for himself. She didn't need to understand his reason for wanting to leave, but "eternum nexus" sounded much more permanent than marriage. It didn't change what had to be done.

His expression remained the same as he began to collect the fabric from her. She waited for his eyes to meet with hers before she subtly nodded. He froze for only a second, taking in the gesture before turning away and out of the room. And now it began.

*****

"How is Fallon doing?" Lauren asked Quinn once she was safely back in her room later that evening.

"Better. She is focusing on this Erebus situation. There isn't much to find, and nothing names him specifically," he admitted.

"He's different than the others. It's not just his royal status. He understands some of my needs."

"In what way?"

"It sounds weird to you, but not all blood tastes the same. Obviously, I'm not speaking from experience apart from Taylor. But there is a difference. When I mentioned it, Erebus took a greater interest in me. I don't think it's something other Bellators notice."

Quinn changed the subject. "Speaking of your needs. When do I need to send the next batch of blood?"

"After tonight, you won't have to anymore. I'll be free," she said.

"Free?"

"Elijah and I are getting a place together. A nest of our own. I won't be watched as closely there," she explained.

"You're joking. How did that happen?"

"I wouldn't tell Fallon, but we're getting married in a few hours. It's a strategic alliance, not a romantic one. It will provide us both with what we need," she said.

"What happened to you and Taylor? I thought you were together."

"Oh, ummm… no. We aren't… weren't…" She stumbled over her words. "I'm different, ya know?"

Wisely, he stayed quiet over the line. "So… marriage? You're not even twenty-one yet."

"Again, this isn't about love. Bellators don't feel such things."

"Still, is this what you really want?" Quinn pushed.

"Want isn't a choice here."

"So… tonight then," he said.

"It could be worse, Quinn. At least Elijah treats me well and with respect."

"And Taylor is okay with this?"

Lauren sighed heavily, trying to think of a response.

Quinn filled the silence. "It's not my place, I know, but it's more than obvious something is going on between you two. Friends who make out when they think no one is looking usually is a basis for that."

*He had seen us?* Lauren wasn't exactly sure how to feel about that. It didn't change where she and Taylor were, though. "He knows already. He told me to do what I had to do to survive."

"I don't think that marrying a Bellator is what he meant," Quinn said. "Just talk to him before you say 'I do.'"


*****


With her hand tucked in his, Elijah guided Lauren to stand before Raeffe, Barbara and Erebus. The physical display was enough to silence the room.

"Your highness, I have made the proposition to Lauren to commit nexus eternum. She has accepted," Elijah stated.

The silence was charged by the sheer surprised expression on Erebus' face. Raeffe appeared disgusted but said nothing. Lauren let out the breath that she hadn't realized she was holding.

"The ceremony is not to be taken lightly," Barbara warned. "Are you certain that this is what you want?"

Lauren didn't miss that she was only asking Elijah.

"Yes, Elijah," Raeffe added quickly. "There is no need to make haste here. Especially with the upcoming mission. It is imperative that you guide the warriors to safety."

Lauren lightly gripped Elijah's hand, concerned by Erebus' continued silence.

"The importance of the mission and my role within it are not in question," Elijah replied calmly.

"And when do you presume to have the ceremony?" Barbara questioned further.

"Tonight would be ideal," Elijah said confidently.

"That would not be possible. It takes time to set up and prepare for the ceremony," Barbara stated. "As I am departing this evening on my own mission, the ceremony will have to be delayed."

"After successfully completing my last mission and receiving acceptance from Lauren, I took it upon myself to get everything needed as to not put undue burden on the nest. We all have our jobs to do here and to do them well. There is no need to take up more time than is needed for the ceremony itself," he said.

Raeffe looked to Erebus for confirmation of rejection. He was clearly in a losing battle with his temper. Lauren hadn't realized how important a role Elijah truly had within the nest. He was the second in command at the nest after Raeffe.

Erebus looked between the two of them. "I would never deprive Bellator law. I would only caution this action should both parties not be fully educated about what it truly means. And all that comes with nexus eternum."

Elijah nodded. "She is aware of the consequences of all aspects."

Erebus stared at Lauren for a long moment before standing to his full height. "Then there is no further discussion needed. The ceremony will take place in five nights' time due to Barbara's schedule. When she returns to the nest, the ceremony will proceed. Congratulations to you both."

Elijah gripped Lauren's hand as they thanked Erebus and began to walk slowly out of the room. Her chest felt tight again. She couldn't really understand the depth of this decision. She looked back towards Erebus as he finished whispering to Raeffe. His eyes locked onto hers in such a fierce manner that she almost walked into the door on the way out.

*****

Lauren fidgeted with the hem of her sleeve as Elijah walked beside her. "There's something I forgot to mention about nexus eternum," he said.

"What?" she asked, already nervous.

"We already discussed the physical part of the ceremony. While emotion isn't something that we show as Bellators, it is something we all feel minimally. Once we are linked together, you will have access to my emotions and I to yours. This access is to assist while on missions to seek the other's health, etc."

Her heart began to race in her chest. "If you thought I was strange before, it will only get worse now."

He grabbed her hands to stop her fidgeting. "It isn't like that. We will have to adjust to it, but it won't make me think lesser of you. And I don't think you're strange."

"Then why did you wait to tell me?" she asked.

"I had to tell you everything, but I know how much you overthink things. This new information will not be enough to change how you already feel. You and I will be one in a few days."

# Chapter Eleven

Lauren's door opened not long after she had returned to her room. Barbara entered, and without a word began to remove Lauren's "décor" from the room.

"What are you doing?"

"Moving you."

"Where?" Lauren pressed, needing more information. "The ceremony isn't until you come back."

Barbara didn't bother looking at her as she continued to put her things into one space. "If nexus eternum is definitely going to commence, there is no need to wait until the ceremony to get you settled into living quarters."

Lauren assisted, grabbing up her things and packing them up into her duffle bag quickly as Barbara wasted no time walking out of her door. Lauren followed her down the stairs and down the hallway, past the meeting room where she'd just addressed Erebus. Her focus hadn't been on trying to explore this hallway at all.

Barbara turned down another corridor and stopped at the first room on the right. She didn't bother knocking, heading right inside and placing Lauren's decorative items on a desk by the window. Lauren couldn't believe her eyes as she entered the room.

The walls continued the marble design, however, the lower portion of the walls continued the wood panels. There was a closet and dresser of dark wood, in a sleek modern design that her room hadn't come with. The ceiling was light grey with a black veiny design threaded through it. But that wasn't the main focus of the room.

A massive four-post bed adorned with the same purple and green colors from the meeting room greeted her. Lauren's duffle bag slipped from her fingers as she took it in. There must have been a mistake. There was no way that this was her room. This much she was sure.

"Where are we?"

Barbara stared at her with a mixed expression. "Your new living quarters."

"Lauren?" Elijah asked, entering behind them. "What is this, Barbara?"

"Per the request of the king, due to the conflict of schedule only, you may proceed with nexus eternum formalities until I return for the ceremony."

"Erebus moved me," Lauren concluded.

Elijah stared between both of them until Barbara took her leave. Lauren didn't know what to say in the empty silence. Elijah wasn't serving up any explanations, either. She glanced down at her duffle bag on the floor, wanting to grab it and go back to the holding cell. The urge was strong, but she knew that it would be frowned upon, especially since this was the king's order.

"This isn't exactly what I had in mind," she began. "It's a nice change of venue, though."

He closed the door, giving her his back. "Whatever you're thinking, don't. You're not free yet."

"I said 'yes' to your proposition. I won't leave you at the altar."

Elijah shook his head, although she noticed the tiny smirk straining to hide upon his lips. "There is no altar where we are concerned."

"Don't crush my dreams so soon. A girl only gets married once," she said in a sarcastic tone.

He grabbed her bag from the floor and took it over to the closet. "We can keep this in here for now. It's only a few days."

Lauren agreed as she fought to contain her yawn. The tiredness seemed to be hitting her all at once now that she had had the meeting with Erebus. She'd have already been asleep had Barbara not moved her out of the room. Now she had to figure out what to do. Sleeping with Elijah seemed to cross a line in her book.

"Go on, get in," Elijah encouraged, gesturing toward the bed. "I have to go on mission tonight."

"A new one?"

"Yeah, but that comes with the territory of being promoted," he said.

"Promoted? To what?"

"Nest Leader."

"Oh, fancy. Do I get a title, too?" she teased.

Elijah ignored her comment as he pulled out his leather jacket from the closet. He pushed back his dark hair, eyeing her dubiously. "What's wrong?"

Lauren shrugged uncomfortably, keeping her expression neutral. Her concerns were only beginning to bloom with all the changes. And even though she'd made her choice to proceed with nexus eternum with Elijah, her heart was screaming that she was losing her way.

He walked over to her side, gesturing between them. "Nothing is going to change here, okay? I know this is a lot to take in, but we have to do this."

Lauren nodded along, biting her tongue.

"I promise you, everything will be all right. We will be out of here soon. I will be out until morning, so get your sleep."

She couldn't be positive, but it was almost like he was trying to say something without saying it.

*****

Elijah had not been joking when he said that he wouldn't be back until the morning. And even then, he had walked in by the nick of seconds on the clock before it struck noon. She had arrived back into the room only minutes before or she would have missed his entrance. His eyes were tight, tension rolling through his shoulders making his back stiff.

The urge to touch him overwhelmed her senses. Only fear kept her feet planted by the window. She watched his breaths struggle to stay in control for only a second before she was in front of him. She carefully began to remove his leather jacket as he grunted uncomfortably.

Whatever he had seen had left him unable to speak about it. She was certain he was trying to hide what he'd been through. There was only so much she could do with the limited information she had about the missions. Lauren closed her arms around him gently just in case he was hurt.

"Close your eyes and relax," she whispered. "You're home now."

He kept his silence, although she felt his muscles slowly loosen up. She escorted him to the bed, pulling back the covers only to tuck him in once inside. He closed his eyes and rolled into the pillows. Part of her wanted to stay with him to be there if he needed anything. Another part wanted to get some answers about what he'd been through.

Nexus eternum was new for both of them, but space was something she respected. He needed to process and breathe on his own for a little before trying to speak with her. It made perfect sense. She wasted no time quietly walking back to the desk to grab her hair tie to put her hair up into a messy bun; training was scheduled regardless of her status upgrade.

"Laur—" Elijah sighed gently.

She blurred to his side, only noticing that he'd already passed out. But she was almost certain he'd called her name. How strange. She stood there for a few more seconds when he took a deep breath, sinking farther into the bed.

Lauren stood between Jon and Alan, another Bellator. Jon slowly approached in his usual technique at the same time Alan began. She couldn't use the technique she already learned with multiple attackers. She had to draw on her existing training and improvise to best suit this situation. The issue was her brain was still focused on Elijah back in their room.

The more she tried to focus on subduing one, the other would claim her, but thinking outside of the box was what she did best. She battled against Alan as Jon approached from a new angle. She anticipated his arms wrapping around her and instinctively knelt down out of reach between both of them. She swung her leg out and around, tripping Alan before popping back up and focusing on Jon.

His expression was neutral but the tiniest hint of surprise was in his eyes. He again tried to parlay with her until Alan made his approach upon her. This time instead she grabbed Jon's arms, spinning with him, allowing Alan to end up attacking his partner.

"What are you doing?" Alan asked.

"Improvising. I'm guessing that humans won't exactly be coming after me in our battle technique."

"And if you were to fight another Bellator?" Jon pushed.

"They wouldn't expect it, either. Does that happen often? Bellators fighting each other?" she asked.

"It is rare, but better you're prepared," Alan stated.

"Do female Bellators fight?"

Jon glared at her insinuation that the training was pointless. "Back to training."

"Females are pretty rare... What would the punishment be for taking one of our lives?" she asked anyway.

"Ask the king. He'd be the one to order it," Jon said.

Lauren thought that through as she continued her training. After the look they'd shared, she wasn't sure how Erebus would respond. When they were alone, he seemed like a normal Bellator, still trying to make it and gain support from his fellow warriors. He didn't put on a show. That was reserved for the nest.

Alan took initiative by beginning the Bellator dance in her direction. She battled him for space, but he wouldn't retreat, only stealing more as she reluctantly stepped back. It wasn't until she was backed against the wall that her frustration began to show on her face.

He pinned her with his forearm across her throat. This had been reminiscent of what had happened that night with Fallon. She furrowed her brow as she pushed off the wall with her legs, forcing his release as they tumbled. Lauren rolled to her side, allowing the momentum to keep her moving away from him until she was able to get on her feet.

Jon made no move to join, only watched from the corner of the room. Her instincts were telling her to bolt from the attack. What did that mean? She was a Bellator. Fighting was what she was made for.

Alan glared at her from a crouched position, waiting to spring at her. She couldn't explain why she did what she did next. It all happened so fast. One minute, she was ready to run, and the next, her teeth were bared in his direction. Her instinct took over, and she was on him, hands pinning him to the mat with her teeth a millimeter away from sinking into his throat.

Her fingers curled around his shoulders with a tightening grip. There was a strange warmth inside of her with every moment she stayed poised to strike. A very small, dark want was eclipsing her brain function. Just a thin string was keeping her in place when a shadow covered them.

"Good restraint," Jon complimented. "That is all for today."

Her brow furrowed as she tried to release Alan. She hadn't really wanted to hurt him. It was only training. She could let him go now. The trembling in her arms and hands gave her away. The struggle was more real than either warrior thought.

"That is all," Jon stated firmly.

Lauren pulled back from Alan's neck as the trembling spread through her. Alan carefully moved aside as she tried regaining full composure. The intensity of the urge to attack was more than she expected would be within her. And from the looks upon the warriors' faces, they thought the same.

Lauren had tried to shake off the overwhelming feelings, but even a cool shower didn't help. Her fears of what was really hidden within her were slowly taking root. She had underestimated herself from the beginning, partly from denial... okay, entirely from denial. She knew who she was and refused to allow the monster within her change that. The only problem was, she was more monster than maybe even she could handle.

When she approached her living quarters, the urge to knock overcame her. The new living arrangement was not sitting well with her. The only thing keeping her from knocking was knowing how strange Elijah was earlier. She didn't want to force him to wake up when he was finally getting his rest.

She quietly went inside the room, only to find him hunched over the desk. His back stiffened as the door clicked shut behind her. She cast her eyes towards the closet and into her bag. She rummaged through until she found the bottle of pills from Quinn. She grabbed two capsules and downed them quickly.

The trembling was slowly subsiding, and the less she had to explain the better. The real reason as to why she'd reacted that way was eluding her, and part of her feared looking too closely for a reason. What if she didn't find one? What if it was simply that she just wanted to hurt him? That wasn't who she wanted to be and would dare not admit that to anyone.

With hope in her throat, she took two more capsules. Her emotions, for once, seemed in check. It couldn't be her new living quarters having this type of effect. Whether she liked it or not, she enjoyed being around Elijah. This had to be different, didn't it? She dumped a handful of pills into her palm and downed them.

"Hungry?" he asked from the desk.

"I'm fine," she said before dumping more pills into her hand. Even if she could leave this nest of demons, it would do her no good. She wouldn't let Taylor see her like this.

"What happened?"

She ignored his question, finishing up the bottle, wishing that the effects would start already. Or even just a taste of real blood. That would block it all out. The pure delicacy of human blood, it was like magic. She could imagine it traveling down her throat with ease.

"What are you doing in here?" Elijah asked from right behind her.

Lauren kept her hands moving about her bag like she was looking for something, allowing the bottle to blend into it. "Can't find my eyeliner."

"So why don't you want to go out to feed? Erebus gave me permission," he pushed.

"Um… Taylor and I are not exactly talking right now."

Elijah looked confused until the light bulb came on. "You told him." It wasn't a question. "You told him about nexus eternum." He shook his head with disbelief.

"It's a big deal, okay? He deserved to know."

"And I'm sure he gave you his blessing," he said sarcastically. "You need to feed."

"Don't push this, Elijah."

"What if you had some leverage with Taylor? His blood for information that would be useful for him?"

Lauren eyed him as she stepped out from the closet. "What does that mean? What do you know?"

Elijah stayed silent a moment, pacing slowly.

"What are you doing?" she asked.

"Trying to keep you alive."

"No games. That is not who we," she gestured with her hands between them, "are."

"Do you believe in me?" he questioned.

Lauren gritted her teeth but nodded.

"Then call him. Tell him we will be there around ten."

She couldn't miss the word 'we' if she tried. This was not going to go over well.

# Chapter Twelve

The engine roared to life like it had a mind of its own to escape. She barely heard Links & Chains playing through her stereo system. Her mind was on full throttle contemplating what they were about to do. She had no idea what Elijah was going to say, and worse, she wasn't sure that Taylor would even meet up with them. He hadn't answered her call, so she'd left him a voicemail.

"How much stuff do you have on campus still?" Elijah asked.

"Well, the majority is with Taylor, although I have a few things at my old dorm. The night you took me, I had brought my academic stuff back to my old room."

"Are you one of those couples that argue non-stop?" Elijah asked.

Lauren ignored his question. "When you go on missions, how do you get to your destination? Walk?"

Elijah glanced out the window, watching the trees pass by. "We have an SUV and go out in groups at a time."

"Carpooling at its best."

The distance seemed to grow between the nest and the campus as she drove. She knew from her last escape attempt, trying to run the whole way back was almost impossible. As she made the last few turns, a memory bubbled up.

"After Fallon confirmed that I'd turn into a Bellator, I ran away... drove away... whatever. I just had to leave. I couldn't accept what she was saying," Lauren explained.

Elijah didn't appear surprised at her admission but kept silent, allowing her to continue.

"Didn't have any idea of where I wanted to go. There was just this feeling—instinct—to drive south—"

"That was your first clue," Elijah cut her off. "You were coming to us."

116

"Raeffe would have had me killed on sight. Even you thought I was pathetic and broken when you met me. You have no idea of what it was like before then."

"You were in transition, Lauren. We would have coaxed you to see that and trained you accordingly until the eclipse," he said.

"Stupid me, I was busy taking midterms," she said sarcastically.

"Denial is the best illusion a human can come up with."

The campus illuminated her vision as she drove upon it and easily found an empty parking spot. She ran a hand through her hair as the familiar grounds wrapped its security around her. It felt so lame that an academic site could produce those feelings, she couldn't deny it.

"Where to first?"

Lauren nodded toward her dorm, which she once shared with her two close friends, Gina and Hilary. She used her badge to buzz into the building. It surprised her that it still worked but, while it felt like she'd been away for years, it had only been weeks. She went up to the room, knocking on the door before going inside.

To her shock, the room was empty of everything. No mattresses, posters, anything. It was like they'd all been erased. She didn't even have to explore further to know her belongings were gone, too. There were only two places her property could be. Either it had been sent home or Taylor had it.

"I need a minute," Lauren said as they left the building.

She rang Taylor's cell phone again without success. Her fingers curled around the device as she began to pace. Was he more upset than he let on about the nexus eternum? It wasn't like he didn't understand that this was about survival. Maybe she was overestimating how much he really could handle.

Her thoughts flew back to when she was training with Jon and Alan. They were preparing her for a fight she was not ready for. At any level. She truly needed to be prepared for herself. The pep talk, she had hoped, would give her the courage and inner strength to push through, but as the trembles began to roll through her frame, her fears became real.

The reason behind the fear was becoming clearer and her emotions were starting to get the best of her. She turned the corner, leaning against a building to keep Elijah from stumbling upon her. She took deep breaths to calm down, but it only seemed to make the trembling worse. The training had ripped open the scabbed-over emotional wound of the initial attack. The attack that changed her life forever.

It was crazy to think that she'd been able to get over it. Even as pissed as she was that it had happened, it was still a traumatic event that haunted her. She could spout off at Raeffe and Elijah as much as she wanted about how it went down; those memories were trapped inside her mind and wrapped around the veins beneath her skin.

"There you are," Elijah said, coming around the corner.

Lauren quickly spun, giving him her back. "Let's go. He's not coming."

"But—"

"Come on," she said, walking faster towards the parking lot.

She grit her teeth, trying to breathe slowly as they silently made their way through the campus. The darkness of the night was a benefit she appreciated. Her emotional state was becoming increasingly unstable the farther they walked, and the shadows were helping to conceal that. Her vehicle sat patiently awaiting their arrival, which only made her feel worse knowing that she was going back to the nest.

"You're not one for being quiet. What is really going on?" Elijah pressed.

"Nothing."

Elijah stopped behind the car. "Is this about him?"

"No."

"I can't help you if…" He stopped speaking before walking closer.

"You're unsteady."

Lauren grasped for the car door handle. "I'm fine."

He came over to her side, blocking her path inside the car. "No games. No lies. Are you *that* hungry?"

"I'm not hungry," she huffed. "You're getting as bad as everyone else."

Elijah placed one arm on the car door and the other on top the car. "We're not leaving until you've fed. I mean it."

Lauren looked into his eyes, the shadows overtaking half his face. Even in the dark, as annoyed as she was with him, she saw the protectiveness in him. She truly wasn't hungry at all and feared sharing her personal life with him.

Bellator life wasn't filled with hugs and memories. Elijah knew who she was more than anyone in this new life; but her capabilities were still in question. And with the knowledge that her life force could take out the nest, she wasn't sure when that would come to be utilized.

"Please believe in me, Elijah."

"I do," he said, stepping out of the way to close the door firmly behind him. "Let's go."

He grabbed her hand and began to blur away with her. It took her a moment to realize what was happening as she ran with him. He was much faster than she would have given him credit for. His grasp released as they passed through an overly wooded area until a small cottage broke through with dark brown accents running through the beige design.

Elijah placed a finger to his lips as they approached. Her chest began to tighten with every step closer. He crept up beside the window, peeking in before waving her over. Her stomach began to clench uncomfortably as she joined him.

He pulled her in closely, leaning into her ear. "She's in there."

"Who?"

He only shook his head as he encouraged her to look into the window. Her fingers gripped the ledge as her legs pushed her up to look inside. There was a living room, sparsely filled with a couch and recliner. A TV played loudly, echoing around the empty room until Lauren saw the woman enter.

Her hands were filled with a mug of hot contents, maybe tea. She placed it upon the coffee table as she sank graciously onto the couch. Her blond hair was wrapped neatly into a bun exposing the slim column of her neck. Her smile was paper-thin as she enjoyed her TV show, sipping at her mug.

Lauren began to crouch back down beside Elijah when her legs gave way, and she fell to the ground. It was her. Taylor's mother. Without mistake or confusion. She was just as she remembered her from their childhood. *What was she doing here?*

Elijah grabbed Lauren up, scooting into the brush before heading back towards where they'd come. She couldn't even speak about what she'd seen. Taylor's mother had been such a huge taboo, and here she was this whole time? She'd abandoned Taylor, leaving his father to raise him and his brother. What was she thinking?

As they approached Lauren's vehicle, the thoughts were no longer in her mind. "What the hell was that, Elijah? Do you know her? Did you know? All this time?"

His green eyes widened in surprise to her onslaught of questions. She paced, not able to look at him. She couldn't calm down. She couldn't even process it. Her breaths were coming in quick succession, and she was losing control. Before she realized it, her teeth were slowly making an appearance, wanted or not.

"Lauren," he said carefully. "What are you doing?"

"Shouldn't I be asking you that?" she asked darkly.

"She was stalking the campus. I hadn't noticed right away. I thought she was taking night courses or something. It wasn't until she started asking about you that I took notice."

"Me? Why me?"

"Again, she wasn't a focus. She'd seen you around with him. When you disappeared from campus, her interest sparked," he explained.

"What does this have to do with anything?"

"She's my mission." His tone said it all.

"No. No, you can't!" A growl she hadn't realized rumbled through her chest. Her eyes glared, as she was unable to resist side-stepping him.

"Stop." Elijah blurred towards her, trying to grab a hold of her. She ducked out of his reach, prepared in her crouch to spring. He hid his surprise of her speed almost perfectly. She allowed her teeth to extend fully with her eyes locked on his. There was no mistaking the gesture for anything less than a threat.

"Over my dead body," she said.

"You've got the fever," Elijah said, staring at her. "I should have realized."

"There's nothing wrong with me, but there will be plenty wrong with you."

"Are you listening to me or just talking through the urges?" he asked. "You were due for a mission to let out the aggression. Why do you think I brought you with me?"

"To take my aggression out on Taylor? Or worse, *his mother*?" Everything he said was making her angrier. It was slowly taking her over more than she realized. She'd never allow anyone to hurt Taylor. He was the one person she'd kill for. That thought stopped her dead in her tracks.

Her teeth began to recede as her breaths came jaggedly. The adrenaline shook her form worse than before. His arms went around her waist, pulling and holding her up. She leaned her head against his shoulder, trying to figure out what had happened.

"I've got you," he said, holding her tightly.

"I… I don't—"

"It was a trigger. Just relax for me," he coaxed.

Lauren couldn't stop the flood of thoughts and emotions. The urge to cry hit her almost as hard as the realization that she couldn't control herself like she thought. It wasn't like her protectiveness of Taylor was new, but her determinedness and excited enjoyment and pleasure was. She was against hurting people. She was! And Elijah, her soon to be other half, almost got the worst of it.

She clutched tightly to him, burying her head into his neck. "I'm sorry."

"It's our nature. Don't apologize."

"But you and I are different," she mumbled.

His sigh was silent but she felt it against her. "No, just you are."

She squeezed her eyes shut tightly against the words. *How different can I possibly be?* She drank blood, she was aggressive in nature and unable to be with the ones she loved. She was a Bellator.

"You can't hurt her," Lauren said. "Please." He stayed silent as he slowly began to let her go.

"Please, Elijah. There is so much wrapped up in this that you don't understand. Human problems, not Bellator," she stated.

"If I don't complete the mission, you know who will."

She swallowed hard, knowing it would be Raeffe without question. Her mind flew through scenarios. There had to be another option that Elijah wasn't seeing. He took a step back, but she followed him, keeping her arms wrapped around him.

"I want her for myself. How wonderful of you to find exactly what your future wife needed to survive," she cooed cryptically.

"As long as I'm not on your hit list."

Her turn against him was still sending trembles through her frame. "You know that I care for you, right?"

His eyebrows rose with suspicion at her admittance. "You do?"

"Yes. Just don't threaten people I love, and we will be fine."

# Chapter Thirteen

"Would you kill me if ordered to?" Lauren posed the question to Elijah, keeping her eyes forward but watching him with her peripheral vision.

"You were on the approved kill list only for a short period of time. You're trainable, sneaky, female and now officially spoken for. You're very much safe," he said.

"Great, but that's not what I asked," she pushed as she drove back towards the nest. "Would you kill me?"

He glanced out the window, taking his time to answer. "What do you think?"

"You would follow your orders," she said, pushing her hair back behind her ear.

"Would you kill me?"

"Only if you were trying to kill me," she said. "Do you mind if I disappear for a few hours tonight? I promise to come back to the nest tonight."

"I don't think so."

"I know where Taylor is. You wanted me to feed," she pushed. "And you'll know if I haven't fed. Better than anyone else would."

He didn't respond, but she was certain he would agree to it. It wasn't much longer before she pulled into the parking lot. He still hadn't agreed, but she took advantage of it. She slipped out of the vehicle silently and began to head towards the woods.

"Lauren…" he called after her.

"Cross my heart, I'll see you soon," she said before blurring away.

Her speed was shaky at first due to the fever attack she had earlier with Elijah. She kept her thoughts focused on Taylor. He was the reason the fever broke. He was like the calming balm to her soul… when they weren't fighting, at least.

The cabin appeared in the darkness as dim lights shone in the window. Her resolve was slowly crumbling the closer she got to the door. Her hands shook as she rapped on the door. The footsteps were almost silent from her side of the door—almost. The door slowly crept open and dark brown eyes gazed back at her.

She went inside, kicking the door shut behind her as she wrapped her arms around him. "You have no idea how good it feels to see you."

He held her with one arm, making sure to lock the door behind her. "I wasn't sure I actually would see you again."

"You've been trying to get rid of me since we were little," she scoffed half-heartedly.

"And here you are, despite everything."

Lauren stared up into his dark brown eyes, wanting nothing more than to get lost within them. She could feel his heart beating against her chest as she soaked up the feeling of his closeness. Maybe the Bellators were wrong; maybe she was the addictive personality. Part of her wanted to devour him in one slow, burning bite.

He leaned down, closing the space between them until their lips met. She moaned aloud into his mouth as his grip tightened around her waist. Her patience was non-existent. She wasted no time, pushing his back against the wall and climbing up his frame. His strong arms held her as she wrapped her legs around his waist as they welcomed each other fully.

His taste was unlike anything she could ever imagine. His touch was like ice, sending shudders through her to calm the flames that wanted to burn her down to ash. She was utterly shocked when her back hit the couch; she hadn't even realized that he'd moved them.

"You drive me nuts, do you know that?" Taylor said, standing beside the couch.

Lauren blinked up at him, still in shock. He'd dumped her onto the couch. "What?"

"One minute you're so concerned about our friendship that you won't even share a bed with me. The next you tell me that you're marrying *Elijah*." He glared at her. "Now you're all over me like you can't get enough."

"I know, I'm sorry. You're right," Lauren said, sitting up. "I haven't been myself lately."

Taylor sat down beside her. "We need to talk. I want you to tell me what's been going on with you. But I need you to tell me… Are you seriously going to marry him?"

"Is that a deal breaker for you?" she asked cautiously.

"You asked me if I loved you, followed by 'oh, by the way, I'm going to marry someone else.' What deal did we have there, Lauren?"

"An honest one," she replied, staring at the floor. "It was stupid of me to put you in a corner like that. Really, I am sorry."

"Would there be another option for you to choose even if I had said what you wanted to hear?"

"Unfortunately, no. There is only one option available to keep me safe from Erebus. That would be to marry another Bellator—"

"What does that mean?" he pushed.

"Elijah and I could move to a nest of our own to train Bellators to protect themselves. I've been in training since I've been back. It would continue in our own nest, except we would not be under anyone's thumb."

Silence stretched out between them as she gave him more time to devour the information.

"Do you love him?" Taylor asked.

"That is such a human concept to be put in an unrealistic situation. Love doesn't exist in the Bellator world."

"Bullshit."

"It's true," she said. "What I feel is foreign to anything they could

126

even think of. I'm not like them."

"Then answer me," he pushed.

"I do care for him. He protects me from the others," she replied evasively. Taylor silently stared until she relented. "No, I don't."

Taylor stared down at her. "Will he touch you?"

"Not the way you do. It's strictly business between us. He is very respectful of me, and he knows of *our* relations. I wouldn't be here now if he didn't allow it."

"Allow," he said with dry humor. "He has no idea what a handful you can be."

"Oh, he's catching on, trust me," she said with a soft chuckle. "I answered your question, but will you answer mine?"

"Well, we could talk some more or…" He leaned in, nibbling into the crook of her neck.

"You don't fight fair," she complained as he snaked his hands into her hair, pulling her lips against his. She allowed him to take advantage for a few seconds before she turned her head away, breaking the kiss. "It's only me, Taylor."

"I know, and because it's you, I know you'll understand," he said, continuing to kiss up her neck, "without words."

There was no hindering their noises as they danced the fine line that she knew all too well. Her mind struggled to concentrate as he continued to give her not only what she wanted, but what she needed. His fingers set her skin on fire as his lips chilled her to the bone. It was heaven and hell wrapped in one as she cried out to be saved.

Lauren began to pull away, trying to remove herself from his actions that had her flying towards cloud nine. She knew the plummet all too well.

Taylor breathed heavily, confused by her actions. "What? What's wrong?"

"We can't do this, Taylor."

"Do you know how long it's been?"

"That's the only reason? Because—"

"I want you," he said, cutting her off. "And you want this," he continued, lightly brushing the back of his knuckles down her ribs.

"I…" She shivered at his touch. "I want—"

"Me," he finished. "You want me. Now let me have you."

His touch was no longer light but determined to stoke the fire she'd tried to tame. He kissed her, quieting any rebuttal she could have made.

"This isn't you," she complained against his lips.

He continued to kiss down her neck. "Yes, it is. This is me with you."

She tried to clear her head as he nibbled and kissed her into further confusion. "You're on my mind, in my dreams, everywhere I look."

Lauren moaned softly between his words and caresses. "This isn't happening. It's a dream…"

Taylor cupped her face with both of his hands, forcing her to stare into his eyes. "This is what we should have done when I finally got you back weeks ago. What I should have said to you when you asked me if I loved you."

She could easily see how hard it was for him to bring it up.

He grit his teeth for a moment. "No one gets me like you do. Even now."

"You don't have to explain. I get it. Honestly, I do."

His eyes softened. "No, you don't. You will one day, but until that day comes…" He leaned in until their noses touched. "I'm not going anywhere, Lauren."

She lost the ability to speak for the second time. He would be with her? He would stay? Her mind drummed up a million questions in a second, moving too fast for her lips to speak aloud. "We're in this together," he clarified.

Lauren sat there stunned, mildly watching him take in her mental process. *He was with me.* Her emotions ranged from happiness and excitement to fear with everything in between. This was what she wanted, more than she could imagine anything else. He nodded as confirmation to make it sink in.

She went to him then, giving of herself what he wanted just as much as she. He took his time with her, unlike before, making love to her in ways he never expected.

*****

Curled up in his arms, he nuzzled her cheek, placing kisses. "I do love you, Lauren." She looked up at him as he spoke. "I didn't want to admit it, especially before we slept together, but I do."

She felt weak from his words, he knew her too well.

"Do you need to go back now? You can't wait until morning?"

"It is morning," she laughed, slipping her shoes back on. "I don't want to start a panic."

"Before you go, one more thing."

"What's that?"

She saw his gesture as she blinked before the blood erupted from his hand.

"To keep you going."

Her hesitancy was gone; she cradled his hand as her tongue lapped at the wound. Her feast was almost as musical as their own entanglement. There was nothing more she wanted than to stay in this moment with him forever. The tiny cabin was a safe haven; neither of them expected to come back after he brought her here to transition the night of the eclipse.

129

"Are you still hungry?" Taylor asked.

"I'm more refreshed now than I've been in months. Thank you."

"Does *he* know you're here?" Taylor asked.

"No, I can't allow anyone who could harm us to know this place exists. Just in case we need a temporary hiding spot."

He nodded an understanding as she wrapped his hand in gauze. She grabbed her jacket, donning it just before she headed for the door. Leaving his side was getting harder and harder over time. She knew one day she wouldn't be able to do it. And for both their sakes, she hoped that day was not any time soon.

"I have to head home to check on Dad and see what trouble my brother has gotten into while I've been away. My phone will be on, so call when you can."

"You didn't get my calls earlier?"

"I will make sure it's not on silent like earlier," he said. "Let me know if anything changes."

Lauren nodded as he unlocked the door. He placed a chaste kiss upon her lips one last time.

"Be careful," he said.

"Always."

\*\*\*\*\*

Elijah appeared much more lively upon her approach towards her vehicle. His jacket was thrown over the trunk of the car as he practiced his training. She smirked beside herself as she caught him mid-advance unexpectedly and caused a rumble to come from his chest.

"Hey."

"Hey yourself," she chuckled. "Ready for a good morning sleep in?"

Elijah nodded, grabbing his leather jacket as they made their way into the nest.

They both stopped at the front door, noting the warrior blocking their way. "Erebus requests your presence."

Lauren wanted to turn and run at the sound of that. They had been out all night long, which Erebus obviously already knew. Either he was scoping for results, or he had changed his mind about allowing Lauren out. For some reason, she was certain his summons had to do with putting more chains around her.

Erebus had made no qualms about how important it was to be loyal to the nest as well as not putting their way of life in danger. She'd done neither of those things that he could be aware of. She glanced toward Elijah who nodded, proceeding inside. Her skepticism lessened as there was no escort to the meeting room.

Elijah went on inside as she meandered behind. She had to tuck her happy memories away to keep up the normal facade. It wasn't until she approached Elijah's side did she catch on to the extra tension. Erebus' face was like stone as she'd ever seen it. His eyes were cold and determined.

"We've lost a warrior unexpectedly," Erebus began. "We will need another to take his place. Raeffe will be on mission to find him."

"Who?" Elijah asked.

"Alan, as of last night, disappeared from the nest," Erebus stated, this time his eyes landing on Lauren. "Jon and you were the last to see him."

Lauren held her tongue as her eyes flicked towards Elijah. "Oh?"

"It is rare for a warrior to leave without notice. So I spoke with Jon," Erebus hinted. "And do you know what he advised?"

She could only imagine what Jon had said. He couldn't understand where her aggression came from or why she reacted the way she had during training.

131

What could he truly have said? However, if she were in real trouble for anything, there would be Bellators all over. Lauren shook her head in response.

"Jon complimented your basic training and stated that you were ready for the next level. That is very out of character for Jon, let alone for any Bellator to level up this quickly."

"Jealousy?" Elijah inquired. "Alan can be quite a handful when he wants to be, but I've never seen him react like that."

"You and Raeffe both, Elijah," Erebus continued.

The picture was slowly taking shape before her. She was getting pegged as the reason for Alan's disappearance. Not that she was surprised that she would be the one to take the fall; but she was surprised to hear Alan had taken off.

"Lauren, do you have anything to offer?" Erebus asked.

She shook her head, deciding it best to stay silent.

His cold stare wouldn't relent, stretching the silence as he stared her down. She only stared back, blinking innocently. Part of her wanted to stick her tongue out at him and blur away childishly. She knew better than to dig a hole that deep, though.

Elijah cleared his throat, breaking the awkward silence. "Your highness, we both have just returned from mission and are depleted on our energies. Maybe with some rest, we can be of more help."

Lauren took that moment to agree with a nod and hopeful eyes.

"Sleep well," Erebus said, although his eyes mocked them.

She tried her best not to walk too quickly from the room, but as soon as she was out of the door and turned the corner, she bolted for their living quarters. The second her feet reached the room, she felt Elijah on her tail. He shut the door, locking the handle right behind him.

"What does this mean?" Lauren asked straight away. "For Alan, I mean.

Is he a deserter?"

"Raeffe is on the hunt for him now. There is no deserting the nest."

"He's on the run for his life now, isn't he? Erebus wants him dead," she stated.

Elijah pushed further. "Are you going to lie to me too about what happened yesterday?"

She shook her head as she sat on the edge of the bed. Starting at the beginning of it was easy; hiding the truth was much more difficult. The training exercises she explained without details, but the attack on Alan, even without the details, sounded horrible. It had been a senseless fit, too. She couldn't even look at Elijah as she spoke, unwilling to say more than what she already had.

A look of frustration and helplessness mixed upon his face. "Get in bed."

"What about you?" She didn't want to sleep with him, but he was just as tired as she was. That much she knew.

"I have to speak with Jon. He knows more than he's said to Erebus. And I can't imagine what Alan would have been thinking to cause him to leave," he said.

"I was horrible, Elijah. Worse than horrible, much worse than what happened between us last night. I can't be sure that Jon knew I was going through the fever or if he actually thought that he had broken through the humanity inside me."

"I'd guess the breakthrough since he complimented you to the king. Of course, he was selfishly taking the credit. I wouldn't expect any less," he said, tossing his jacket on the back of the desk chair. "Rest up, we're gonna have a busy afternoon."

*****

133

She had no idea how she managed to fall asleep after everything, but her mind had called it quits within a half-hour. Her dreams were empty and airy like they were filled with something she couldn't see or grasp. The pressure of the bed dipping beside her only barely grazed her consciousness. She had no recollection of when Elijah had left it.

The light was dim, hidden behind the trees of the late afternoon. Her arms and legs tingled with aches as she tried to gather herself up to full awareness. Movement by the desk caught her attention—Elijah's hand writing out a letter. His dark hair was damp from a fresh shower, curling around his ears.

"Are you awake now?"

Lauren stifled a yawn and stretched carefully. "I guess so."

"Raeffe and I are switching off. I won't be back tonight."

"Is my training cancelled then?" she pushed.

"Yes. Instead, you must assist with bundling and dispersing the clothes today. I figured it would keep you busy and in the eye of multiple Bellators."

"You're worried about me," she said.

"We're not married yet, Lauren. There is only so much power I have, especially in this nest. Only a few days now."

He stood up to leave, grabbing his jacket, when she flew out of bed at him. Her actions were uncoordinated and faster than her thoughts. She grabbed his jacket from his hands, tossing it on the bed.

"You have to mark me in some way as your betrothed."

"What?" he asked.

"Humans have engagement rings, even boyfriends give their girlfriends something of importance to show off that she is off the market," she explained. "I'm going to wear your jacket. It will smell of you and keep the others away."

"We're not dogs, Lauren. I don't have to piss on you like you're my territory. This was an equal agreement between us. Bellator law won't be threatened, even in the early stages."

Lauren glared. "You just don't want to give me your jacket."

He smirked against his will. "Damn right."

*****

Her activity for the afternoon was as boring she knew it would be. She grabbed the clothes and sorted them out into sizes like Barbara had showed her. A piece caught her attention, a dark t-shirt without any rips or stains she could see. The tag identified it was just Elijah's size, and she put it aside for when he returned. Her focus returned to making sure everything was perfectly placed, and as the warriors came in, the distraction was exactly what she needed it to be.

Group after group came through as she handed out the garments. She kept a steady pace that left no slack until she had to grab the next bundle. Her ability to blur was a benefit in the sense that she was able to slip down the hall and into the walk-in pantry without anyone taking notice.

She grabbed two big bundles and tried to push the door open wide enough to squeeze through without any success. She put one down before putting the other outside into the hall. As she leaned down to grab the second bundle, a broom fell down from behind the door, clanking loudly. Her heart stopped as a small squeak slipped from her lips.

"Fudge-o-lees," she complained, before picking it back up.

She sat it back against the wall from where it had fallen when she noticed scratch marks in the wood grain. She remembered humans had been held within this room before, but something about these scratches was making her nervous. The closer she inspected the wall, the deeper the marks seemed

135

ingrained. Like it wasn't humans who'd made them...

"Ahem..." A throat cleared in the doorway. "Aren't you supposed to be down the hall?"

"Grabbing reinforcements," she stated, not bothering to look to see who'd spoken. She grabbed the second bundle and almost dropped it when her eyes met Jon's. He seemed less than thrilled at her nonchalant response, even after seeing it was him. He hadn't been warm or comforting towards her once, even during training. She certainly couldn't understand his interest now.

"Are you Barbara's permanent replacement?"

"Nope," she said shortly. "Care to step aside so I can finish my assignment?"

His jaw ticked to the side as a slow smirk revealed itself; it was more menacing than she expected it to be. His normally neutral facial expression was all she truly knew. The last thing she needed was for him to think that they were friends, or worse, that she was weak enough to be bullied.

Lauren moved forward, pushing past him while taking note he hadn't offered to grab the first bundle. She leaned down, tugging up both bundles together, keeping her focus on getting back to the room down the hall. She noticed the next group of warriors was just arriving and got back to work separating the clothes into sizes as they approached.

Her thought of wearing Elijah's jacket flicked through her mind. It seemed he had more faith in the warriors than she had. Jon certainly wasn't interested in her, but he was looking for something. She already knew how selfish they could be. No wonder she stood out here.

# Chapter Fourteen

The heavy knock on the door came unexpectedly early. She sat up in a rush, startled as her hair flew forward past her shoulders. Her head began to pound intensely as she gripped the sides of her head. She could only squint as her eyes refused to open all the way.

Lauren pushed herself out of bed, allowing her feet to shuffle towards the door. The irritable face on the other side of the door was an unwelcome surprise. Raeffe's dark eyes sent a shiver through her as did the impulse to slam the door in his face. She leaned against the doorframe, trying to appear more awake than she was.

"Where is Elijah?"

Lauren squinted from the loud volume of his voice. She glanced back towards the bed and found it empty, apart from where she had been all night long. He hadn't come back.

"He went on mission last night," she said.

"Did he not return?" His concern was making her more attentive.

"I passed out. I don't really know," she said, gripping the sides of her head again. The more she spoke, the worse her head felt.

"What's wrong?" he asked.

Lauren took two deep breaths and tried to shake it off. "Nothing. I must have slept wrong."

"When he returns, have him report directly to me."

She shut the door, slumping against it as she looked back towards the bed. It seemed so far away from where she stood. She shuffled her feet back towards the bed, tumbling into it, allowing her body to rest further.

*****

The banging on the door woke her up violently. Her stomach clenched tightly as she felt the pulsing in her head. It was like someone had driven a knife into her skull. She rolled out of bed, only barely standing as she leaned forward and fell into the door. She tugged the door open slightly not noticing anyone there.

What the hell?

Lauren opened the door further, sticking her head out to check the hall, finding Jon walking away. That couldn't be good. She shut the door, looking back towards the empty bed. Where was Elijah? Just the thought of him sent a zinger through her skull.

She crumbled to the floor with her hands around her head. *What is with this stupid headache?* It couldn't be that she was hungry. She had just eaten recently. She had gone a lot longer without eating before now and hadn't gotten this pounding in her skull.

Elijah mentioned he wouldn't be back right away, but it was way past normal check in time. Especially if Raeffe had checked to see if he had returned, which was also strange. She crawled over to the desk and grabbed her cell phone. No missed calls, and the time said four in the afternoon.

She noticed a small piece of paper that had her name scrawled upon it in Elijah's handwriting. She flipped it over, noticing instructions.

*Take two drops from the black bottle in your bag in the closet. If your head has already begun to hurt, take four drops.*

Lauren froze in place. *How would he know that my head would hurt today?* He must have been writing this yesterday afternoon when she had awoken and seen him at the desk. *Did he do something to me?* The confusion wasn't helping the throb in her head. She went into the closet, finding the bottle easily enough. She unscrewed the top, noticing the clear liquid in the dropper.

Her loyalty to him wasn't in question aside from this strange psychic knowledge. She couldn't for one second doubt that he would hurt her without it coming from Erebus, and as of now, she was still in the clear. She lifted her tongue, allowing four drops into her mouth before closing the lid and putting it back into her bag.

She went back to the desk to continue reading his instructions:

*If the headache does not recede within the hour, alert Erebus to your fever. He will make sure you are properly taken care of.*

**Do not trust anyone.**

The last line sent a shiver through her. It hadn't really hit her that she only really trusted Elijah. And he wasn't here.

It had taken more like three hours for her headache to finally calm. She had made the decision to not see Erebus about it. She accepted his headache time frame, but she'd had a bulging migraine by the time she read the note. And the last line was haunting her. Even Erebus apparently was on the list of people to watch out for.

Leaving the living quarters scared her more than it ever had before. She couldn't be sure if it was because she didn't trust the Bellators or herself. There was no way she could stay cooped up in her room, though. Old habits were going to have to die hard now. And there was one place she wanted to check.

*****

Lauren knew that moving around at night would be way too obvious if she were caught. She needed a good cover story to keep herself unattached and flexible. With Elijah's warning in her mind, she slipped out of their living quarters.

The hallway was just as quiet as if it were late in the evening. No Bellators were meandering the hallways, but that kept her on her toes as she turned the corner, headed towards the front door. Her suspicions only grew as she noticed that no one was posted at the door. She glanced around and still saw no one.

She picked up the pace down the corridor towards the pantry before going into it and shutting the door behind her. She turned on the light and took a closer look at the marks on the wall. Her first assumption that it wasn't human was confirmed by the depth of the marks. The first day of training had showed her how strong Bellators could be.

The only Bellator being threatened as of late was her. And she wasn't the one who made these marks. There was mention of a traitor whom Erebus had exposed personally. She wondered what more information she could get and from whom. Slipping out of the pantry, her destination was set.

Lauren went back to the front door and leaned against the wall, checking down the hallway towards the meeting room. There was not a single Bellator in sight, not even to protect the king. Her nerves were already on edge as she advanced towards the door. She stared at it for a few seconds before crossing her arms over her chest and heading back towards the meeting room.

She knocked once and entered the great room. It was empty apart from the king himself, sitting upon his "throne," staring back at her in concern. She stopped at the entrance; mostly from shock of seeing another Bellator in the nest. She stupidly had expected him to be gone since everyone else was.

"Oh, hi."

"Is there something you needed?" Erebus asked. "Since you feel right at home letting yourself in here."

"I was nervous," she admitted.

"What do *you* have to be nervous about exactly?" he asked coldly.

"Elijah's been on extended leave on mission," she said. "My training was called off today for obvious reasons, and I'm…" She couldn't appear weak in his presence, not completely. "…irritable."

"Ahhh," he said, leaning forward in her direction. "You miss him so

140

soon?"

She stood her ground, keeping the distance as her safety blanket. "Elijah is a great warrior. He is strong and independent while staying loyal to his nest. I can only hope to bring such honor within our own nest."

Erebus eyed her from his seat. "Why are you here, Lauren?"

"What is the punishment for a Bellator taking the life of a female Bellator?"

His nostrils flared ever so slightly that she would have missed it if she weren't paying such close attention. "Have you been threatened?"

"No," she began. "I was training with Jon and Alan when the question came up. I figured we were training against humans alone. Apparently, I'm being trained to protect myself from more than only them."

The intensity of Erebus' stare didn't alleviate in response to her answer. "If any Bellator were to endanger you or Barbara, the punishment would be swift."

Lauren glanced down at the floor. "You'd kill for me?"

"Yes." His voice was strained. "What kind of king would I be if I didn't?"

She nodded, trying to keep calm.

"Is Jon training you well?" Erebus inquired.

"He pushes me to do what I didn't think I could."

"And Elijah has assisted," he pushed.

"He has lent his talents when requested."

Erebus nodded as if he expected the answer. "You'd prefer Elijah to train you…"

"Oh," she said. "Jon has been a good trainer so far. I don't know if I am ready to be at Elijah's level of expertise."

"Have you no confidence in yourself, Lauren?"

"You mean, am I suicidal? Because going up against someone at level hundred after only practicing in the mirror is exactly that." She shook her head, realizing that she was getting nowhere fast with him. "I have confidence in what I know."

*****

She headed back towards her living quarters more than a little irritated when she caught sight of Jon stopping by her room again. His face was the usual neutral mask he used in training, but training was off until Barbara returned. *What is he doing here?* Dodging him wasn't going to get the answers she was looking for.

He turned away from the door, walking back down the hall from which she presumed he came. Instead of calling after him, she followed him down and around the corner to another set of stairs. She followed him up as he stepped inside his own room, shutting the door.

Her self-preservation instinct warned her to go back to her living quarters. Stalking another Bellator was not on the approved activities list by Elijah, for sure. But her instincts told her to do it anyway. *Why have instincts if I'm only going to ignore them?*

She didn't bother knocking on the door but pushed it open and stepped into the doorway. Jon was busily hovered over the desk, scribbling angrily until he stopped suddenly and looked back towards her presence. His expression remained blank, not confused at all to see her.

"You were expecting me."

"No," he replied. "Have you seen him?"

"Who?"

"Close the door," he said.

Lauren couldn't force herself to leave, but being alone in his room with him was too much. There was a chance that after all the training they'd done,

142

she'd surprised him, maybe, but impressed him? Not even close. And like she'd just said to Erebus, she wasn't suicidal.

"Not a chance," she said, looking back towards the hall. "I thought you wanted to tell me something."

"Why would I want to talk to you?" Jon asked, increasingly impatient.

"You're looking for Elijah. He's not back yet."

His features became more menacing. "He's left, too."

"On mission," she replied automatically, but this time she heard the emptiness around it. He wouldn't have taken off, especially after Alan left. He'd never desert the nest he was so loyal to, would he? And he'd planned to marry her. That was a huge deal. Not because of the marriage portion, but because they planned to escape the nest and disappear for good.

Elijah had spent too much time putting all the pieces into place to just leave. She couldn't accept that as even an option. He was a true warrior and would keep his word to her. The trembling in her fingertips was the only hint that her body was disagreeing with what her heart told her. Elijah wouldn't abandon her, too.

# Chapter Fifteen

Lauren gripped the tops of her boots as she slid them on. She rifled through her duffle, locating the slim, rectangular box Quinn had given her the last time she'd seen him. As she opened the box, the shimmer of a small dagger with a razor sharp blade greeted her. She grabbed it, slipping it into her jeans pocket where it fit perfectly. Her determination grew as she collected the cell phone and tucked that into her other pocket. Her patience level had disintegrated after speaking with Jon. She would not wait for Elijah to come back. What if he didn't plan to, or worse, couldn't?

The only way to get the answers she needed was to leave. Permission be damned.

Lauren grabbed her jacket, tossing it on as she proceeded out of their room and down the hall. She didn't slow down as she passed by the meeting room or when Raeffe crossed her path by the foot of the stairs. Her fingers gripped the front door handle and twisted it with ease as she proceeded out of it.

"Get back here!" she heard Raeffe demand in the background, but she kept moving. This was her mission. She would do what she was supposed to, and that was to make sure all the warriors came home safely. And she was going to bring home hers.

"Lauren!" Raeffe shouted from behind as she blurred into the woods.

*****

She waited until she was a few miles away before pulling out her phone to check in with her friends. She couldn't speak to them. They would hear the worry in her voice, and that wasn't her intent. She texted instead.

*Hey, Quinn, have you heard from Elijah lately?*

His response came a few minutes later. *Not since the other day. Why?*

*Let me know if he reaches out.*

She searched the immediate area for any sign of Elijah. She even took a stroll by the cabin, only to find it empty. Taylor hadn't come back yet, and for once she was glad that he wasn't nearby. The disappearance of Elijah was making her skin crawl with every second that passed.

Her search was short lived without taking her car. After this adventure, she could imagine ending up back in her holding cell as punishment for leaving without an escort. The more she thought about the stupid rules they foisted upon her, the more she lingered, defying her tiredness, but soon she decided it was necessary to return back to the nest.

Elijah he said that he would've been dropped off for a mission. Her anxiety had sent her off without the few details she needed. Unfortunately, the only person who had direct contact with him was the one eyeing her as she walked back towards the front steps. His dark eyes were glacial.

Listening to any of Raeffe's reprimands were off the list. She cut him off before he could even begin. "You were the last to see him before he left on mission. Where was he headed?"

"I don't think your concern is in the right place. You defied the king's command."

"The king understands loyalty to the nest. Especially when it comes to the second in command in this nest," she stated. "How would it look to lose two Bellators in one week in his presence?"

Raeffe stood his ground. "The king is waiting to speak with you."

"I'm sure he's asleep by now."

"The king does not sleep," he said matter-of-factly.

"Ever?"

"Never," he replied, ushering her inside. "Young and clueless."

Lauren felt more than ready to take on the world as they approached the meeting room. Her reasons were justified in her own mind. Maybe she was getting more sure of herself, but the threat of Erebus was having less and less of an effect on her. Maybe she was reckless after all.

"As you requested," Raeffe stated to Erebus, entering the meeting room with her.

Lauren went right up to stand before the throne with an irritable expression. "Here I am."

"That will be all, Raeffe," Erebus said before turning his attention on Lauren. "Defiance is not becoming of a warrior."

"I wouldn't classify myself as a warrior just yet. That would mean I actually did something other than playing house," she said. Reckless wasn't as strong a word as she needed.

A humorous expression lit his face. "Are you feeling the pressure? It's the only explanation I can think of for which you'd dare speak to me in such a way."

"If you knew who I truly was, what type of person I am, then you wouldn't be asking," Lauren replied, staring him in the eyes. "I am certain that there is nothing surprising about me other than the fact that I have a mind of my own and a loyalty like no other."

"Loyalty, huh?" he replied sarcastically. "Do you think I am blind to what is going on here? Why, all of a sudden, after being in this nest for such a short duration, you're suddenly betrothed to a warrior with actual power?"

She glared, wanting to spout off at him but knowing that what he said was true apart from her intentions. "If I were betrothed to you, would you expect any less of me? I would be out there looking for you. Not sitting here twiddling my thumbs, handing out garments like a maid." Lauren closed her eyes as her head began to ache. "Your highness, if you are willing to kill for us, why wouldn't I do the same?"

The sarcastic humor left his face all at once. "You're serious? Send an untrained, volatile and distraught warrior out there on a mission? Ask me again why I wouldn't think that to be ludicrous."

"Ludicrous or not, you can't deny my trying to find Elijah won't hurt our cause. Even if he and I were only nest mates—or whatever term used here fits—I'd want to get one of our best back on our side."

Erebus stared blankly at her as if she'd not spoken. She could see by the determined expression that he wasn't going to let her go freely. She'd have to just keep finding ways to escape, but there was such distaste in the act. She'd never had to sneak out of her parents' home.

"Am I to be punished then?" she pushed.

"I haven't decided yet. Probably."

Lauren shook her head, allowing her distaste to show. "I guess I'll have to wait for him to come back to me." She sighed, turning back towards the door. "I never expected to be abandoned twice, but I guess I can't count on anyone."

*****

Lauren paced her living quarters as questions overran her mind. *Where the hell is Elijah? And Alan, for that matter?* Barbara had taken off just before everything has gone to hell. *Is she part of this? Is this some type of distraction to keep everyone's focus away from the real issue?*

She skimmed through the papers on the desk. Not one piece of paper spoke to her. No details of where Elijah might have gone, even to find Alan. She couldn't ask Raeffe, but an idea started to form in her mind, and she knew exactly what to do.

Her fingers punched in the numbers to call Taylor. If she accomplished what she thought she would, she wouldn't be able to reach out to him for a while. She could only hope it was only a little while.

"Hello?" he answered with a rough, sleepy voice.

"Sorry, I know it's late. I need you to stay away from here for a while."

"Is something up?" Taylor asked.

"Elijah has gone missing. And I'm going after him. I won't be around to see you, and things might get bad around here. I'd feel better knowing you were home."

"Where is he?"

"I wish I knew. But someone does, and they're doing a hell of a job keeping that secret."

"You shouldn't do this alone," he said.

"I'm not planning on it. I can't say much more. But I wanted you to know, just in case."

"In case what? You're disappearing?" he asked, this time with more concern.

"I have to. Only a short while. I will find you. No matter what."

"No, don't—"

"I have to go. Love you," she said before hanging up and turning off the phone.

*****

She packed her duffle bag with every item that belonged to her and trashed what she no longer cared for. She grabbed a few things that clearly belonged to Elijah and stuffed them in before zipping it up. Her head throbbed slightly, the drops doing little to help. Not that she understood what she was taking. That little fact did not escape her.

With the lights off and her courage at maximum capacity, she slipped out of her room. Careful to make sure no one was in sight, she repeated her escape route towards the front door. Again, no one was standing guard, and she double-checked to see if anyone was watching from the top of the stairs.

Her intentions were clear as she pulled open the door, but she was halted in her tracks. Jon was posted on the steps, staring out towards the front yard. She stepped out, placing the bag down before shutting the door behind her. He glanced her way only for a second before facing the yard again.

"If you're smart, you'll go back inside," he warned.

"Are you going to stop me?"

"It's my job specifically to keep you from leaving," he admitted, completely at ease.

She rolled her eyes, tossing her duffle bag to the bottom of the steps. She was leaving one way or another. It was his choice to move aside or be pushed aside. "Asking you nicely isn't going to work, is it?"

Jon glanced down at her duffle bag and back at her. "You can give it a whirl if it'll make you feel better."

Lauren took a step towards the edge of the front steps, and he blocked her way easily enough. It wasn't that she didn't want to try, it was more that this was wasting precious time and energy. This game wasn't worth it.

"Who put you up to this? Raeffe or the king?" she asked.

"Doesn't matter."

"Yes, it does. If it was Raeffe, I can easily get through you," she replied.

"That almost sounds like a challenge."

Jon knew nothing about her except when it came to their training sessions. He had no clue what she was capable of. And maybe she didn't, either. She slid her hand into her jeans, tugging out her gifted dagger and aimed it at her heart.

His eyes scanned the yard once more before he noted her stance. "Is that all you've got?"

"It's all I need," she stated, shoving the tip into her skin with a gasp. "Let me pass… or else."

"You're not going to do it," Jon stated uninterestedly even though he couldn't take his eyes off of her actions.

"Well, I'm not staying here. Either you let me leave, or I find a new way out," she said, pushing harder until the sharp tip of the dagger broke her skin, allowing some of her black life force to expose itself upon her shirt.

He reached for the handle as she shoved it in a bit deeper. "Stop."

"Not until you back down the stairs."

The struggle between getting his way and risking her existence warred upon his face as he slowly back down the stairs but blocked her way from going down them. "There is no way that you can go out there already injured. Wherever you were headed isn't worth it."

"Elijah is out there, and he is worth it. I'd go through far worse to bring him home," she said, nodding for him to step out of the way.

"Elijah?" he asked. "Raeffe is already out there looking for him and Alan."

His response led her right into what she already knew. "Are you going to deny my right to find my other half?"

Jon's face became stone as he fumbled for a response.

"Elijah and I are betrothed and will be one when Barbara returns. Erebus has already congratulated us," she pushed. "Now get out of my way."

Without losing eye contact with him, she kept one hand on the dagger at her chest and grabbed up her duffle bag with her free hand, slowly making her way to her car. She unlocked it, focusing on getting the bag into the backseat before getting herself inside. She wasn't stupid. The second she removed the dagger, he'd be right there to grab her.

She took a slow, deep breath and slid inside the car with the dagger still in place. Jon began to walk towards the car, but she felt safer inside the vehicle. It roared to life as soon as she turned the key. She would have to remove the dagger soon; driving like this might seriously impale her. Already, the pain was getting to her.

She slowly eased the dagger out of her skin. The minimal wound left behind wouldn't last long. She punched the gas as she spun from the property, leaving Jon in her dust. Raeffe would find out about her escape soon enough and be on the lookout for her. That only made the urge of her to find Elijah that much stronger.

*****

The drive toward the campus had her hoping for a miracle. She couldn't think of any practical reason to find Elijah there at all, but it was where they had 'met,' maybe a hundred times before she actually knew who he was. It was where her life had turned for the worst, and he had kidnapped her himself back to the nest. It was a place he felt comfortable being, which explained why she also felt the same.

As she parked the car and began to walk the grounds, she felt in her bones that he wasn't there. Still, she took her time to walk around and check every crevice that she could, just in case. He couldn't have just disappeared into thin air. He couldn't have… faded away.

Lauren blurred back to her vehicle, trying to ignore the frantic energy clawing its way through her chest. She knew little to nothing about his missions apart from stalking the campus. That was when her mind clicked to the most recent adventure.

Her breath became erratic at the thought of him going after Taylor's mother. It was even worse because she had begged him not to. Maybe it had something to do with that. She couldn't think any further on it as her hands automatically drove the car in that direction. She drove with a determination that she hadn't felt since her instincts were telling her to go back to the nest that first time.

Had Elijah betrayed her trust and gone back to complete his mission? He had never answered her when she asked if he would kill her if ordered to. She had assumed that he would have. He was loyal to his nest, and he knew them much longer than she did. The only thing that could save her was the fact that he was trying to get away from them and take her with him.

She pulled over to the side of the road, parking the vehicle behind a few overgrown bushes. At least this would buy her time from being found by anyone else. She scrambled through the wooded area the same way Elijah had taken her. The windows were illuminated a dull bluish color, beckoning her to check inside the house.

Her eyes scanned the surroundings as she approached until she peeked through the window like she had last time. There Taylor's mother sat, grossly taken in by a movie playing upon her TV. She was alone inside, surrounded by the minimal furniture and floor lamp. Lauren's worry only settled a bit as she stared at the woman.

His mother appeared so comfortably at ease in the little home she'd made for herself. Lauren didn't know why she had deserted her family. If Taylor knew the reason, he hadn't shared it even after all these years. Lauren continued to watch her as she leaned into the cushions of the couch contentedly, surrounded by plush pillows as her blond hair wrapped around her shoulders and cascaded down her back, seemingly oblivious to the drama she had caused when she ripped her family apart.

All Lauren could think of was the pain that she'd unknowingly, or maybe even knowingly, foisted upon both her children without a second thought. Marcus, Taylor's brother, was still acting out, no one even doubting that it all reflected back to feeling abandoned by his mother. Lauren couldn't mentally process how hurt Taylor had been, how angry he was at the time and still was when it came to her. Knowing that she was so close and still not willing to confront him made Lauren want to bang on the door herself.

Before Lauren started a fight that she couldn't finish, she took a slow, deep breath to shake off the trembling that urged her so strongly to go after Taylor's mother. She turned back from the house to go back to the car. It was safer for them both, and certainly better for Taylor, if he took care of this personal situation himself. If he chose to, anyway.

She was almost past the small backyard area when she noticed something odd in the snow-laden ground. It was dark, almost like an animal had made lazy burrow too close to the surface of the ground. The closer she approached, the bigger the dark mass became with only a small gleam from it, shining in the moonlight. *What could possibly be out here this late at night?*

# Chapter Sixteen

Tiny, little circular drops led her closer to the dark mass, increasing in size as she approached. No animal could have made those marks in the snow, not even tiny bird feet. Nothing was matching up, especially when two long, dark jean-clad legs came into view. Whatever hesitation that had kept her advancing slowly disappeared within the instant she noticed the leather jacket. She ran full speed toward Elijah's body.

"No," she whispered softly, as her hands frantically grabbed at his shoulders. He made no movement at the sound of her voice, which frightened her further. She rolled him over to his back, removing the snow that was stuck to his lips and face. His skin was pale and cold to her touch. "Oh, no... no, please," she said, trying to shake him.

She noticed the tiny circular drops surrounding them. She had mistaken them for some type of footprint, but she was wrong. It was blood. His blood. There was no mistaking their life force for normal human blood. She leaned down, placing her ear down towards his nose. Feeling just the barest hint of breath gave her hope.

"Quinn," she said into her cell phone, her actions moving faster than her mental state. "I need you and Fallon."

"Do you know what time it is?" he complained.

"I've found Elijah's body. I can't..." She tried to take another breath as her fear caught up to her adrenaline. "I won't let him die."

"Where are you?" Quinn asked as she heard him moving about through the phone line.

"I have my car. I can meet you guys wherever you think will be safe for both you and him."

"All right, head to the highway heading south," Quinn advised.

Lauren glanced at Elijah again, only minimally daunted by trying to move him by herself. She couldn't trust any Bellator to help her. Not with this.

"Text me the address, and I'll meet you there."

"Okay, see you in a few then."

"Quinn," she said quickly before he could hang up.

"What is it?"

"I'm gonna need blood."

The line stayed silent for a beat before he responded, "See you soon."

As she carefully slid her hands beneath Elijah's armpits and began to tug him across the yard, her level of confidence began to wane that she'd make it the distance to the car with him in one piece. She found a nearby tree, hiding his body beneath it before retreating to her vehicle. She drove it as close as she could manage without hitting a tree or making it obvious to Taylor's mother that she was on her property.

The backseat was empty apart from the duffle she'd thrown in it. Moving that to the front passenger seat, she went back to work, tugging Elijah's body across the snow, careful not to hurt him any more than he already was. Lifting him up was a Herculean feat that she couldn't believe. Halfway through, she swore that she'd drop him back to the ground but held on for dear life. His dear life.

Her worries were just as vital after shutting him into the backseat successfully. Trying to find her way back to the road and to a destination that she was unsure of concerned her. She checked her phone for the address and put it in her maps option for directions. She gave Elijah one last glance before hitting the road.

"Stay with me, Elijah."

*****

Pulling off of the highway and down a few back roads, she was concerned that he'd not moved at all. She found the driveway easy enough with Quinn flagging her down. She pulled alongside the curb and unlocked the door to the backseat.

"What happened to him?"

"I wish I knew for sure, Quinn," she said.

Quinn opened the car's back door and felt for Elijah's vitals. "The door to the house is open if you want to go inside."

"I'm not leaving him," she stated, going to the door to help remove him from the car.

Getting Elijah out was much easier with Quinn's help. They took it slowly up the driveway and into the ranch style house. She followed Quinn's instruction down the hall and down the basement steps. They went into an open and lit bedroom, lying Elijah down on a comfortable looking bed with pillows set up for easier breathing.

Lauren searched Elijah's face, wanting him to peek open one eye and stick his tongue out at her like it had been one bad joke all along. But as she took in how still he was, how vulnerable he truly appeared in his unconscious state, the more protective she felt. This was no accident that she'd stumbled upon. He had been attacked and left for dead.

"Rehabilitating a Bellator isn't part of who you are. And I can only imagine how Fallon is dealing with this, but…" Lauren looked up at Quinn with the intensity of a thousand pack of wolves, "Elijah is mine. He will survive this because there is no other option."

"How long was he out in the elements?" Quinn asked, deciding to ignore her threat.

"I'd have to guess between one to two days at most."

"He's healed up from the initial wounds," Quinn said after removing Elijah's leather jacket and shirt.

The planes of Elijah's strong chest were clear of blemishes and tense with muscle beneath a layer of thin, dark chest hair. His stomach was flat, minimal hints to the abs beneath the skin, but still unmarked. For once, she was annoyed by the healing ability of their condition.

She glanced down at her shirt, still sliced through from her own self-inflicted injury. "Where's his shirt?"

Quinn handed it over, and she quickly opened it up fully and gasped aloud. The holes were only in the back of it, sliced up to six different times from different angles and depths. Her hands began to tremble again, knowing what he had endured. Whoever had attacked him had been a coward to hit him from the back without giving Elijah a chance at a fair fight.

Fallon came into the room silently with a black backpack over her shoulder. Lauren crumpled the shirt into her hands to disguise the slices in the fabric. Quinn pulled out a few metallic looking items from the backpack as Fallon sat by the desk. As he assembled the few pieces, Lauren no longer had to guess what it was. She turned away as Quinn took an alcohol swab to Fallon's arm.

The room was like stepping into a past that she had not known existed. Maps, both national and international, crowded the walls of the room. Post-It notes were strategically placed by certain locations noting castle tours, zip-lining and scuba diving spots. She hadn't imagined Elijah having normal hopes and dreams for his future before he was turned into a Bellator.

She ran her knuckles gently down his cheek, remembering how he'd been the one to watch over her. There were so many times he could have walked away and left her to the monsters within that nest, but he hadn't. As much as he protected his sister, he had made it his priority to care for her, too. That only made her chest ache further seeing him like this.

"He's going to need more blood," Lauren said.

"This will have to do for now," Quinn replied, switching out one full tube for another empty one.

"How long can he stay?" Lauren asked.

"How long do you need?" Quinn asked.

Lauren faced him while eyeing the silent Fallon. "Minimum three, four days if at all possible."

"Two it is," Fallon stated firmly. "He wakes up, he leaves."

What other choices were there? She had two issues at hand and only one that was within her control. Lauren nodded an acceptance before going to Elijah's side. She brushed her fingers through his hair gently before leaning in.

"I have a mission, Elijah," she whispered softly. "My mission is to hunt down the monster that did this to you and end their existence. Only when that is accomplished and we can be safe, will I come back to you. I promise to make them pay."

She kissed his cheek, allowing the last remnants of her kindness to seep into it. That was when she let it all go. The trembling slowly began to travel through hands, her arms and shoulders. She grit her teeth, pulling her hair back into a tight bun as she headed for the door.

"Feed him much as you can manage."

"Where are you going?" Quinn asked.

"To kill the bastard who did this."

*****

All she could hear was the roar of the engine as she drove down the highway with one destination in mind. One of her favorite Links & Chains songs blared from the radio. She flipped it off firmly. She couldn't bear the idea of listening to her favorite band with such putrid thoughts running through her mind. It would ruin Links & Chains for good, and she wouldn't allow the Bellators to take that remaining piece of happiness she had. The memory associated with her future plans would be silence.

Lauren pulled the car off to the side of the road, grabbing the dagger, the blade of which was still covered in her life force. She took a collective breath with one thought in mind as she got out of the car and shoved the dagger into her back pocket. Justice eventually came for all, and today, it was her turn.

The sun hadn't even crested, but she could smell the dawn soon approaching. As she reached the nest, another warrior was standing guard at the front door. She could only imagine Jon having to explain to his superior that he'd failed to keep her inside. Maybe she was banned now from returning…

The warrior seemed surprised to see her walk up so calmly. She could tell he was new to this position just based on how easy he was to read. Even as angry as she was, that anger was focused toward a specific party. He stepped aside, allowing her entry.

"Is Jon here?" she asked.

"Yes."

"And Raeffe?" she pushed.

"He hasn't yet returned from mission."

"Thank you," she said, going up the stairs.

As she closed the front door, her instincts began to take over. A countdown was slowly ticking in her mind. She had to make the most of what she had. She went to the foot of the stairs and glanced down the hall to notice still no one watching over the meeting room that held Erebus. There was something strange about that, but she couldn't put her finger on it.

She went up the stairs quietly, making no sound at all. The hall was empty as she expected. The warriors on mission hadn't yet returned, and those left behind were resting. It was a quick, split-second decision as she decided it best to knock on the door instead of rage her way in. And it paid off.

The door to Jon's room opened within a minute, and she pushed her way in, shutting it quickly behind her. Jon stared back at her, slowly gaining his full attention from his half-asleep form. She took a preemptive step in his direction only to watch him twist into battle formation. Apparently, her earlier antics had put him on edge.

"What? No 'hello,' Jon?" she asked mockingly.

"What are you doing here?"

She placed a hand on her chest. "I thought we were friends. I'm hurt."

His chest rumbled in protest. "Did you find him?"

"Yes. What's left of him, anyway."

"Left of him…?" he stated, almost unbelieving.

Lauren took advantage of the distraction, taking a slow step towards him. "His blood stained the snow leading to his most prized possession."

"I don't believe it."

"It was a massacre," she replied quietly, again taking another step until he was within reach. She wasn't a fool. He noticed how close she'd come, but with the softening of her voice, it seemed to him that she was not as crazy as he'd thought. "So what am I supposed to do now, Jon?"

"Alan wouldn't have hurt him. Elijah gave us a lot of shit, but he taught us how to survive." His eyes met with hers. "If Elijah is gone, Alan is, too."

Lauren closed the space between them. "It's been a rough night for us both."

"Why did you come *here*?" he asked menacingly.

"Elijah was all I had. Who else could I turn to who I can trust?"

"Trust?" he asked, this time with anger forming his features.

"I've only spent time with two strong and trained warriors. Would you rather I go speak with Raeffe?" she taunted, dangling the power play before his eyes. "He doesn't care much for me, but I'm sure he can find a service for my talents."

She leaned into his personal space, allowing her body to press up against his, her words forming a new meaning. His eyes grew dark with fierce anticipation although he remained in full control of his actions. With a tilt of her head, their lips were only a millimeter away from touching. She couldn't force this upon him if he didn't truly want it himself.

Jon took advantage, aggressively mauling her mouth in a way she totally understood. He was aggressive and completely in control in every aspect that she'd known him to be. The only weak link in the chain was when she'd taken the option away from him the last time by putting her own existence at stake. And everyone would have blamed him.

"You're dangerous," he groaned into her mouth before nipping his way down her neck.

Her fingers gripped the edges of her jacket, removing it from her shoulders and tossing it to the floor. He took her cue and began to pull off his own shirt quickly. She placed her hands against his bare chest, shoving him back onto the bed before stepping to the edge of it.

Under the early dawn, the sunrays sparkled across her top half as she gazed down at him. She gripped the edges of her shirt, slowly tugging it up and over her head as she stared into his eyes. His eyes drank her in as she slowly kneeled upon the bed, crawling up his frame before settling above him. He wasted no time, reaching up for her face, pulling her in for a deep kiss that allowed another groan to escape him.

As his actions became more frantic and anxious for action, she knew exactly how to calm him down. One of his hands gripped the back of her head, keeping her in place while the other began to grope her body. She kept one of her hands on the side of the bed to steady herself from falling completely upon him while her other one crept behind her back and into her jeans pocket. She carefully removed her trusted friend before leaning into Jon completely, kissing him as deeply as she could manage while sliding the dagger swiftly into his heart.

His body froze completely at the contact.

She pulled away to look directly into his eyes, "Good-bye, Jon."

# Chapter Seventeen

Lauren carried her jacket under her arm as she made her way down the staircase of the nest. She'd managed to take out three warriors in total who were resting, Jon included, although he was the only one she'd had to truly seduce into submission. Taking on Erebus was out of the question. No matter how clever she could be with her female allure, he was beyond those parlor tricks.

She descended the front steps quietly, startling the newest guard. "Oh, it's you."

"Yep, little ol' me."

"Did you find Jon?" he asked.

She nodded solemnly at the ground. "He wasn't very nice."

The guard shrugged. "That's who he is. Don't let him get to you."

"Raeffe wasn't very nice to me, either," she continued.

"Maybe you're a bit too soft. Things are tense around here with Alan missing."

"Maybe you're right," she said, coming to his side to stare out across the front yard. She pulled the dagger silently from her back pocket and slid it into his back, aimed at his heart. He gasped out of shock and fell to his knees before fading into eternity. "Maybe I am too soft."

Her chest ached knowing that the Bellator who guarded the nest had been accurate about Raeffe not being back yet. She could barely keep her teeth from extending at the thought of taking his existence away. Of course, it wouldn't be as easy as Jon or the others. Raeffe would be stronger and smarter. She did have one thing that he didn't, however, and that was the only wild card she could hold against him.

*****

Lauren returned to the cabin and took a hot shower, washing away the memories of that morning. The trembling had subsided only partially, since she knew that she still hadn't gotten to the one she'd wanted. She dried off and dressed in a pair of jeans and a comfortable t-shirt before crashing onto the bed that smelled of Taylor.

It seemed a miracle that she could find such happiness and light while surrounded by such darkness. Even as she increasingly participated in the evilness of her new self, she couldn't allow it to take over everything. She knew that the day that happened, Taylor would be lost to her forever. And he was worth fighting for.

As she lay in bed staring at the ceiling, the need for sleep eluded her. She knew that sleep was a necessary part of the cycle, especially after having such a late night and active morning. And yet it still refused to come for her. She closed her eyes, allowing her body to become relaxed and rest as her mind raced with the possibilities of the day.

The sound of her cell phone going off startled her from the bed. She rolled over, reaching for the device with her fingers. She clicked the accept option and put it on speaker, not yet willing to get up.

"Are you nearby?" Quinn asked.

"Not too far, I don't think. Why?" Her concern overpowered her personal desires for rest.

"His body is not accepting the blood."

"But that is all Bellators consume," she stated.

"I know."

"I'm on my way," she said, hanging up.

She tossed on her jacket and boots, making quick work of locking up the cabin before hopping into her vehicle towards Fallon's. There had to be a reason Elijah wasn't accepting the blood—more than what they could easily deduce. Speeding down the highway, swerving between cars on the road, she made it to the little ranch house in record time.

Quinn opened the door as she approached the pathway. She went right in and down into his basement room. Fallon sat in the corner of the room, silently watching her older brother weaken with every breath. Lauren could see how much worse he seemed even since the few hours she'd been away from him.

She went to Elijah's side, careful not to jostle him on the bed. His muscles were weakening, his cheeks beginning to sink in and his color becoming dull and ashen. He looked much worse than she could have imagined, and she felt helpless to make it stop. She couldn't remove her eyes from his face as she questioned Fallon.

"What happened when he was fed?"

"He swallowed once and then choked it back up," Fallon said in a quietly strained voice. "Nothing else would go down."

"Would a direct transfusion of Bellator blood work?"

"Not a clue," Quinn replied from behind. "I don't have enough to offer him."

"My blood would end him, wouldn't it?"

"Yes," he said. "We're running out of options."

Lauren took a deep breath. "Did you only try Fallon's blood?"

"Yes, the family connection would be a building block for him."

"What if that isn't the case? Try a small dose of yours," she pushed.

"I don't think that is the problem, Lauren," Quinn replied.

"You said you were running out of options. I just gave you another."

Quinn went over to desk with a shake of his head as he prepared a fresh syringe and needle. Fallon only stared from her corner. Lauren couldn't tell heads or tails what Fallon actually thought or felt. She wasn't going to push her, but she was not throwing in the towel by any means. Elijah would be okay.

Lauren watched as Quinn sat Elijah up a bit. He dropped a few drops of his blood upon Elijah's tongue and waited. There was no obvious change that they could see, but at least Elijah hadn't choked on the offering. Quinn waited a few more minutes and still nothing happened. He continued little by little to give Elijah a few drops until Lauren noticed his breathing become labored.

"Sit him up," she said, lifting Elijah's shoulders while Quinn lifted his head and neck carefully. Droplets of fresh, red blood slipped past his lips and down his chest. Her fear was starting to get the better of her. She couldn't watch him like this. Desperation was a dangerous thing.

"I need your blood, Quinn."

His eyes became concerned as they laid Elijah back down to the bed. "You're hungry?"

"Grab a small paper plate if you have one."

Quinn left the room while she went over to the desk and ripped open an alcohol swab, rubbing it against her arm. When Quinn came back into the room, he wasn't sure what she wanted to try, but saw the determination in her eyes and proceeded. He grabbed a fresh needle and syringe, extracting her life force.

"What are you thinking?" he pushed after removing the needle from her arm.

Lauren allowed one drop of her life force to drip onto the paper plate. She took the tube of Quinn's blood and dropped a few drops into it. It began to mix on its own, like the blood was an animated, living thing. She watched her life force overpower the human blood until it all became black.

"One drop of mine and overpower it with human blood. What if that is the key?"

Quinn was already shaking his head. "We're limited on human blood as it is."

"My blood that you used had been starved from the nutrients of human DNA. What if my blood, once I was fully fed, could be the cure for him?"

"And what if you kill him?" Fallon questioned. "Will your experiment with his life be worth it?"

Lauren closed her eyes. "Of course not. I'm just trying to—"

"I know," Quinn stated. "We have to be careful of everything we do."

"Are you fully opposed to a transfusion? If I were able to bring fresh Bellator blood, would it be worth it or a waste of time?" Lauren asked, staring at Elijah.

"We could try to take it slow, but that—"

"Not a problem. I'll be back," she said, heading for the door.

"What do you mean 'not a problem'? Lauren?" Quinn called after her as she hit the stairs.

Lauren made it to the front door before she felt the hand on her shoulder. "What?"

"What have you been doing out there?" Fallon asked.

"Nothing that you haven't done on campus."

"I'm not actively hunting them down. What you're doing is very different," she said.

Lauren smirked, allowing the darker side of her to seep out. "I'm not hunting them. I'm assassinating them."

# Chapter Eighteen

If anyone had warned her a year ago today what her future would entail, she'd have called them crazy. There was no mistake in who she was and who she would continue to be. She was the gleam in her parents' eyes. She was the loyal friend who could be counted upon for anything. She was the A student, never late to class and overly prepared for everything.

She took her time walking through the woods from the cabin, heading directly for the nest. The weight of the dagger, safely tucked into her back jeans pocket, barely registered with every step. The weight of the duty, however, was heavy. She felt compelled and determined to pursue justice in dedication to her fallen warrior. A warrior that had unknowingly touched a part of her soul, kept her in one piece while dulling the pain of the past.

All of the questions and concerns that she once had in regards to Elijah had slowly fizzled out. Whether he had pure intentions while committing her to nexus eternum or not, she was committed to him. Committed in a way that eclipsed her own self-preservation. There was no possible way that she could take out every single Sanguis Bellator in the entire nest; it was only pure luck that she had taken so many that morning. Certainly, they were ready for her now.

And yet, for every step, there was no thought of changing her course. There was no thought of a true plan to execute and find a way to save the life force. The only thing she could think of was removing the threat that constantly put the people she cared about in danger.

The qualities she now possessed were perfectly balanced. She was a unique hybrid of both human and Bellator. She possessed a willingness to follow a path of her own while staying true to her loyal nature. She was trained to be a perfect child, a perfect academic student, and now a somewhat trained Bellator. There was no erasing her ingrained humanity, and that was clearly an issue for the other warriors around her. Especially Erebus.

The sun had ducked behind the trees, ready to set for the evening. She could vaguely see the nest in the distance. No guard was posted from the view she had. Part of her wondered what to expect. Would Erebus himself be waiting for her arrival? Torture was clearly a favorite of his. Would he use the fear of punishment against her?

Lauren kept an eye on the nest for a while, deciding to take her approach slowly and watch for movement. Her cautious attention focused on the front door, knowing there was no other way out. The longer she waited, she knew the worse Elijah became, and that knowledge only gave her more fuel to want to get this over with quickly.

She skirted the woods carefully, steering clear of open areas where she could be spotted. There were no distinguishable footprints that she could see. Finally, amped up with enough adrenaline, she ran to the side of the nest, making her way towards the front step carefully out of view of the windows.

The front door was open. *Not a good sign.* She peeked in, unable to see or hear any sign of movement. She headed for the pantry to use as cover. That was when she noticed the bare shelves. No linens at all. She was cautious going to the training room, but it was empty, as well. *What is going on?*

She went to the meeting room down the hall from the front door and peeked in. Certainly Erebus would be sitting on his throne. But the room was completely empty. Not a sign of furniture or even the wall adornments. Panic hit her chest all at once. They'd up and left without a second thought.

Blurring through the nest and up the stairs, she checked all the rooms but there was nothing left, not even the beds or desks. They'd taken everything. She went into the living quarters she'd shared with Elijah and found a slip of paper on the ground. She knew the handwriting as soon as she picked it up.

*Lauren,*

*Leave this nest now. Raeffe will come collect you tonight at ten at the college campus. You can explain your absence directly to me.*

She was dumbfounded. They'd figured out the nest was under attack and had no idea that it was by her hands. Any humor she would have found in the situation was lost in the fact that Raeffe was coming—and specifically for her. Sure, flirting with a Bellator to distract them had worked, but not with Raeffe. There was no mistaking the hate between them.

This was going to be unlike anything she'd expected.

*****

The cabin was the perfect environment for her nerves. She had the room to pace and blur, trying to work out her concerns until she decided that was getting her nowhere fast. Her options had run out since she had been unable to capture any Bellators to help save Elijah. Dealing with Raeffe was the only option left. And time was not on her side.

She thought back to when she had practiced her training with Elijah. With a deep cleansing breath, she turned to the side, beginning to practice the disciplined footwork. She saw his light green eyes staring right back at her intensely while adding the arms to the movements. She focused on trying to stay in rhythm, her hips doing what they always had naturally. Even as she moved back, his voice penetrated her concentration.

"Less hip movement," he would have commented.

"Yeah, yeah, yeah."

She took the lead, pushing forward and changing the style of the technique to one that fit her comfortably. It was an interesting twist that she'd not thought of before. It was unusual and quirky, just like herself. He would have understood the change, moved along with her. There was no way that he could manage to be at his level of status and not be flexible to change when it was asked of him.

After his missions, he had always come back to the nest. He'd encountered different struggles upon every mission. That was life, wasn't it? Learning to adjust and grow.

With the intensity of her thoughts, she hadn't realized that she'd stopped moving completely. The image of Elijah before her in her mind slowly began to fade. There was no way that she could survive this way of life surrounded by Sanguis Bellators without him. Elijah had become essential to her survival. He was a vital part of the nest under Raeffe's rule, and he deserved better than what he had been dealt. And she would see that he was avenged.

She let down her hair, feeling it wrap itself around her shoulders comfortably as she left the cabin. She got into the car, making sure to roll down the windows to feel the cold night air against her skin as she drove. The roads were easily travelled without the excessive activity of college students during the holiday. Any recollection of the date was lost on her.

Pieces of her human life were steadily disappearing with every new development in her existence. At what point was she considered a full Sanguis Bellator? Would she ever be? There was no way that was her now. She still clearly understood and remembered what it meant to be human, or was that something all Bellators knew but chose to ignore?

Jon and the other Bellators back at the nest whom she had executed without any guilt began to float around her mind. The more she thought of Jon, the less she felt about him. Part of her knew that it was unnatural to feel almost nothing in regards to ending another life, but she couldn't accept how many human lives they'd greedily taken to continue to survive. It was an even trade.

The campus parking lot resembled how it was when she'd left it the last time she'd been there with Elijah. Her temper was aside, at least for now. She climbed out of the car, deciding it was better to walk around a bit so her nerves weren't so tense. Who knew the next time she'd be able to walk the campus like this anyway?

She could see the pathways were cleared for any students staying on campus through the winter break. Even still, the shadows of footsteps were far and few between. And after being here recently with her warrior, she was certain that some of these prints were her own.

Just the thought of Elijah seemed to make the tension worse in her shoulders. She needed to check in; it would settle her to focus. She pulled out her phone, only mildly surprised to see her voicemail box filled up. It had to be Taylor. And with that personal knowledge, she deleted all of them along with the thought of him for the night. Thoughts of him swirling around in her brain were not going to help her tonight.

"Hey, Quinn," she said.

"Lauren," he began sullenly.

"What?"

"I'm… sorry," he said.

Her breath caught. "Quinn!"

"He's gone."

"No…" she whispered as her body became still as stone.

"We tried to give him more blood, but his body was already shutting down."

"Is he… Did he…" She couldn't form the words.

"No, he's still here. He didn't fade away, and I don't really understand why. We won't do anything until you get here."

Just in the periphery of her vision, a tall figure moved within the shadows. She dropped the phone into her pocket as the shadow carefully made its way towards her. She was in shock, she knew that, and knew that no matter what happened now, it meant nothing. Elijah was gone.

Pain screamed from her chest only to short circuit between her heart and mind. The disconnect only left her able to acknowledge the being, now only a few feet away from her. It was like a nightmare that wouldn't relent.

"You're a sight for sore eyes," Raeffe said. "Where's your stuff?"

"I don't have anything anymore."

Raeffe rolled his eyes. "Let's go."

She watched him turn, heading back towards the shadows. "Why would you do this?"

"Do what?" he asked irritably.

"Murder Elijah," she said. "He was no threat."

He faced her then with a scowl. "He's not—"

"I found his body unconscious at his last known mission," she replied matter-of-factly. "He breathed his last tonight."

"I didn't—" he began to protest.

"Of course, it had to be you. I see that now. You were the last to see him when switching the mission that you, for some reason, couldn't complete. And yet, when he didn't return, you knocked on my door looking for him. Like you didn't already know that he didn't come back," she pushed. "There are only three people who know what happened that night."

"Three?" he asked, his attention back on her.

"You, Elijah and me."

Any trace of false innocence slipped from his features. "Elijah can't speak for himself now."

"But I can," she said with a glare.

"You really think that anyone would take your word over mine? If there were any chance of you leaving with your existence intact tonight, that chance has faded away."

"Just like you," she said, making a running attack straight for him.

Raeffe easily stepped aside, ready to take her on. She made quick work of focusing on keeping him in front of her while beginning the battle. He appeared at complete ease as she moved forward, trying to push him back as the trembling rippled through her. She couldn't grab at his arms to disable him since he moved too quickly, countering her movements.

Memories of training against Jon unwillingly started to force their way to the forefront of her mind. Jon was an experienced warrior, but not as experienced as Raeffe. Even training with Elijah had been different. Elijah wasn't truly trying to harm her; this was a battle for her life. A battle to avenge Elijah's death and extend her future.

Within a blink of her eye, he was the one pursuing her. Her footwork became uncoordinated as his approach was sped up, his technique flawless until he had his hand wrapped around her arm, tugging her in and smashing her face into his knee. She used her free hand to grip her face, feeling her life force slowly start to drip from her nose.

She spun out, reaching for her trusty dagger with a determined expression. Raeffe only sneered, waving for her to come after him. She shook her head and nodded for him to come this time. He came hard and fast at her. She only had a split second to drop down and swing out her leg, tripping him up.

Her teeth extended to full battle length, like they had only just realized what was going on. The obvious move was to jump him with the dagger; she knew he was expecting it. Instead, she used the side of the dagger to cut her skin, allowing her life force to cover the blade as well as drip down her arm.

Raeffe eyed her like she was nuts. She fully accepted that notion as she went for him. She used her blade arm, making slashing patterns as if it were a baton with a ribbon on the end. The trembles rippled through her again, while a heavy pant of pain and anger shot through her as she used her unique style of fancy footwork to get close to him.

He would not bend or retreat, only sidestepping before throwing out an arm, grabbing a handful of her hair. She slashed at him with the dagger only clipping his jacket before he rushed her backside, grabbing her blade arm to keep it away from him. Lauren felt his muscled, hard body behind her and felt the superior gesture without needing to look.

With a deep breath and a silent prayer, she used her other hand to grab the dagger, using full force to cut his side. It was quick and superficial, but his reaction was instant as he shoved her to the ground with a release. She dropped the dagger, turning to go after him as he clutched his side. It was there in his eyes that she saw the complete surprise.

She blurred over to him, jumping him to the ground, her teeth ripping into his throat with malice. The life force from her nose had run down her mouth and easily into his neck wound as he screamed out, weakened by her blood and shaking in an epileptic fit. She could only stare at him as his skin began to sizzle and bubble up.

His dark eyes met with hers once more as she gave a subtle nod, like he needed permission from her to let it all go. His face began to relax as the fits began to calm, leaving his limp body still on the ground. There was no such thing as taking a chance. Not when it came to him.

Lauren retrieved her dagger from the ground and returned to his side. "You left Elijah alone to die in the snow. I will not leave your side until you are no more." With that, she drove the dagger into his heart with as much force as she could muster.

He made no sounds, the entire campus deadly silent. Her eyes refused to look away as he slowly began to fade away into the night air, leaving nothing but the sight of her dagger stuck into the snowy dirt.

She was alone, completely and utterly. No one would know what she'd done or what it meant deep down inside. There was no one to go home to; she didn't even have a home. Her world had eclipsed at Elijah's last breath, and the beginning of the end was now coming for her.

**The End**

# About The Author

M. L. Newman is an independent writer who lives in rural Connecticut with her wonderful husband. She is a member of the RWA. She has a bachelor's degree in Social Sciences from Marist College. She is active in community theatre and has played characters ranging from Brigitta Von Trapp in The Sound of Music to Ms. Hannigan in Annie which has inspired the many fun aspects and personalities for the characters in her romance novels.

M. L. Newman is currently hard at work on the third installment to *The Fade Away Series*, but she'd love connecting with you on her Facebook page https://www.facebook.com/pages/M-L-Newman/508027985916037 and on Twitter https://twitter.com/MLNewman1

Looking for exclusive content and more?
Visit www.mlnewmanauthor.com